David Bedford

Inspector ROCKE

"That'll Be The Day ....That I Die"

Table of Contents

Chapter One

My Girl

"Hey, I didn't recognise you with your clothes on Helen," a voice shouted to the pretty nurse as she crossed the room.

"Shut up John," came the swift response, "and stick to playing your guitar, if you've learned how to yet!" John Lennon laughed and mumbled to his friends as they looked on in awe of his confidence with women.

Who would have expected the sound of calypso music to have emanated from the cellar of a coffee club in the port of Liverpool in 1960? The exotic sounding Jacaranda Coffee Club in Slater Street, run by entrepreneur Allan Williams, somehow chanced on the latest thing among the Beatnik world of Bohemian Liverpool.

The club was packed with sweating fans, and a more eclectic, bohemian mix you couldn't have expected to find. Lennon and his small group of art students were sitting over by the wall, keeping their watching distance on a group of Americans. Alongside art students, you would find nurses and businessmen looking for nothing more than an escape from everyday life.

In this dark, damp, pungent atmosphere mixed with sweat and cigarette smoke, a Caribbean steel band is playing an arrangement of "Maybe Tomorrow", the latest hit from Liverpool's new superstar, Billy Fury, still known among his friends as Ronnie Wycherley. The band are the only black faces to be seen in Liverpool city centre, as an unofficial racial segregation was in effect. The large Afro-Caribbean population was   situated within the Princes Road area of Liverpool 8, just a short walk from the city centre.

As the band finished the song, the happy, enthusiastic perspiring crowd made their way up the narrow stairs into the coffee bar area, some clutching a bottle of Pepsi from the downstairs bar, others gasping for fresh air as if their lives depended on it.

Sitting at a table in the window, looking out into Slater Street was a small group of nurses and three American servicemen. Helen, an attractive young lady in her early 20s with blonde hair, still dressed in her nurse's uniform, walked towards the group.

A figure appeared from the basement, a Trinidadian musician, Gus from the steel band, walked the same steps that the nurse had and headed towards Helen's table. He was about 5 feet 10 inches tall, aged 25, who left Trinidad a few years ago and had settled in Liverpool. He saw a group of American soldiers at the table surrounded by some nurses, who were hanging on their every word!

Gus, however, was clearly not happy with the Americans, or with John's comments.

"Hey Helen, is he bothering you," he said, looking in John's direction?

"No," she quickly replied, "he's just one of

those idiots from the art college."

Helen looked in John's direction as she said it, though John just pulled his tongue at her with a grin on his face. She couldn't help but smile a little. Gus, however, was not amused and turned to talk to Helen. Helen sat down at the table with her fellow nurses and, much to Gus' annoyance, next to one of the GIs, Chuck Warshowski.

Unperturbed, Gus tried to spark a conversation with Helen, ignoring the Americans in front of him.

"So Helen, what did you think of our set then?" He waited for some enthusiastic response from her, but he was to be disappointed.

"It was good, Gus," she said, slightly subdued, and with some embarrassment, "but I'm just with my friends." She looked around to those at the table and clearly indicated that she didn't want to engage in conversation with him. As if to annoy Gus and claim ownership, Chuck put his arm around Helen. However, she quickly took it away from around her shoulders, much to his chagrin, and placed his hand back on the table. He, also, was not happy.

Undeterred, Gus pushed on with the awkward conversation.

"That's okay; I can come and sit with you if you like?" The little boyish look on his face, full of anticipation was about to be disappointed again. He even started to move toward the table, but Helen was defiant.

"No, it's fine Gus," she said, holding her hands up to stop him in his tracks. "We are okay on our own, thanks." Helen looked sheepish and wanted to avoid a confrontation with Gus, but he wasn't giving up.

"But I thought we were going out tonight after we had finished," he exclaimed, more in hope than expectation. Helen got upset, and her voice was more annoyed now.

"Not tonight Gus, I've got a headache and just need to get some sleep, so I will be heading back to my flat in a minute," she said defiantly. Gus, like a dog with a bone, tried again.

"But I have been looking forward to this all week," he proclaimed, trying one last time to get his girl away from the clutches of the on-looking Americans. This, however, simply antagonised them, and one in particular.

Chuck Warshowski stood up, knocking the table and spilling some of the drinks. The atmosphere changed in a second and, like that moment in a cowboy film when guns are drawn, everybody stopped talking and looked at the stand-off. Warshowski was over six feet tall, and stereotypically a square-jawed, clean-shaven US serviceman in immaculate uniform. He was from the Deep South of America and his feelings towards his black adversary soon become evident.

"Hey, boy," he said in a derogatory manner, clearly knowing the implication of his choice of words, "didn't you hear what the lady said? She doesn't want to be bothered by anyone, but especially not by some two-bit nigger musician son of a bitch like you! Now get into your banana boat and go back to where you came from and stop bothering the lady."

Helen was clearly shocked and embarrassed by his remarks and tried to hold him back and make him sit down.

"I can fight my own battles, thank you!" she

said emphatically to the American. However, it was too late to diffuse the situation. Gus was infuriated and lost his temper.

"Who you calling a nigger," he screamed, "you lanky piece of white trash. Liverpool is my home, and I have as much right to be here as you do!" Gus was now being held back by one of the patrons, and Warshowski by his colleagues. The two, like proud stags about to fight for their mate, were almost foaming at the mouth.

"Listen, boy," he continued, "you don't belong here so leave these lovely ladies alone."

Gus would not back down either.

"Call me 'boy' one more time and I will kill you....................." There was no more time for words, as a fight broke out between Gus and Chuck as their "seconds" could no longer hold back the pugilists. The doorman had to intervene and nearly ended up with yet another broken nose as a punch just missed him. Chuck's colleagues jumped to his support, and Gus' band mates join in too, but the fight was over as quickly as it started. The opponents stood there frothing at the mouth, but knew it was over, if only for a short time. A rematch was clearly on the cards.

Warshowski straightened his uniform and calmed everyone down.

"Okay, we're all good here, just deal with him and stop him bothering the young lady." With some incredulity, he was trying to claim the moral high ground. Gus wouldn't let him get away with that and protested his innocence.

"I wasn't bothering no one, I was just asking my girlfriend if she was okay."

Helen stood up, clearly wanting nothing to do with either of them.

"I'm not your girlfriend Gus!" she exclaimed defiantly. Gus was almost lost for words.

"But I thought that after last week that we were good?" He obviously interpreted the previous week's liaison differently to the now embarrassed nurse. She sat down again, somewhat ashamed, and, with all eyes on her, knew she had to respond to him.

"No Gus, it was just a mistake," she uttered, hoping for an end to the conversation. Warshowski felt he had to intervene again.

"She's telling you, boy, so get that into your head!" as he pointed his finger provocatively in Gus' direction, the fight nearly started again, and Helen ran out of the Jacaranda in tears. Gus ignored his adversary and went after her.

The crowd inside the club looked through the window and watched on as Helen and Gus had an animated argument on the street, with arms being waved and incoherent shouting seeping through the doorway. Warshowski then followed them out as a taxi pulled up outside the club. Helen climbed into the taxi, quickly followed by Warshowski, who closed the door behind them, and it drove away.

Gus was lost for words and can't believe what has just happened. He slinked back into the club, obviously disappointed, and with thirty pairs of eyes all scrutinising his every move. Nobody said a word. The silence was broken by one of Warshowski's friends, who couldn't miss the opportunity to have a go at Gus.

"See boy, you should stick to your own kind!" Gus hardly lifted his head as he responded.

"Go to hell Yank!"

The other American servicemen were asked to leave by the management, and Gus went back downstairs. As he disappeared from view, joined by his band mates, the jukebox clicked in and broke the silence. It was Buddy Holly and the Crickets with, appropriately, "That'll Be The Day." The irony wasn't lost on the crowd who began to laugh, and the general hubbub started up again, and life continued as it did before.   However, for Gus, silently taking down his equipment, his mind working overtime, replaying the events of the last few minutes in his head, and singing along with the record, "that'll be the day, when you say goodbye, yes, that'll be the day, when I die."

Chapter Two

Another New Boy

Inside the local police station on Hardman Street, the clock struck nine o'clock as Inspector Rocke was sitting behind his desk in his office, working through paperwork. Rocke, approaching his fortieth birthday, was clean-shaven and his Brylcreemed hair was immaculately shaped. He hardly even acknowledged the chiming of the clock as he had been in his office for an hour already. His desk was tidy and organised, though he had a huge pile of papers in his In-Tray. Cigarette in hand, his tie was undone and his jacket was on the back of his chair.

The Chief Constable popped his head in the doorway to break Rocke's concentration.

"Rocke, my office now," Chief Constable Bell barked in his native adenoidal Liverpool accent. Bell, a man whose police career had been spent entirely in Liverpool, in his late 50s, was a chain smoker which showed in his graying beard. His uniform was always impeccable. He liked things done by the book, but saw Rocke as his protege and indulged him his occasionally unorthodox methods.

Rocke, a Liverpool-born son of a Liverpool mother an Irish father is about 6 feet tall, with reddish-brown hair. He had made it to the rank of Inspector and was renowned for getting his man, by often toeing on the very edge of the boundaries as defined by the police force. He jumped from his chair and followed in Bell's footsteps, a man he admired, though he did find some of his mannerisms annoying and his need to have everything documented, a part of the job Rocke hated, sometimes bringing them into conflict with each other. They entered Bell's office, and the Chief took his place on his leather throne behind his huge oak desk.

"Sit down Rocke," he said in a serious manner, which put Rocke on alert. He knew he probably wasn't going to like what was coming next. "Straight to the point," he said, with a hint of hesitation in his voice, "I've got another Constable for you." He sat back for the inevitable argument. Rocke, one of the most experienced officers in Liverpool has had his fair share of rookie detective constables. This was not what he wanted to hear.

"Oh come on Chief," he protested, jumping to his feet. "Not another one! Why is it always me? What lunatic have I got now? I need a detective I can rely on, who will have my back, not another snotty-nosed recruit!" He paced the room as Bell prepared his response.

"Disciplinary issues?" Rocke said with disbelief. Exasperated, Rocke stopped in his tracks and stared at Bell, before sitting down again. "Like what?"

Slightly embarrassed, Bell continued where

he left off, coughing nervously.

"Erm, there was an unfortunate incident with one of the staff from the American Embassy," at which point Rocke stood up again, throwing his hands in the air! Bell was now on the back-foot as Rocke went into interrogation mode.

"And what type of incident was that then," he bellowed, as Bell almost cowered in his own chair? Surely this was role reversal?

Bell coughed again, before revealing more of the story.

"Well, he decided he didn't like him, not necessarily because he was black," he paused, looking for a reaction, "so arrested him and tried to plant evidence on him." Rocke was almost speechless, his face getting redder with every second. "Thankfully," Bell continued, "he was stopped before it got any further and before relations between the two countries were beyond help!" Rocke could hold back no longer!

"So you're sending me a racist bigot to work in Liverpool? Just what I need!"

Bell decided to regain control over the situation. "Sit down George," he shouted, standing up to reassert his authority.

"I know you're not happy, and neither am I, but you know you're the best there is, and he needs a steadying influence like you to get him back on track. He was regarded as one of the brightest hopes at Hendon so let's give him a second chance."

Not a flicker from Rocke as Bell felt he was finally getting his point across.

"And" he continued, "he has been demoted to Detective Constable and put on probation." Rocke sat down again and regained some composure.

"You better be right on this one, sir, because I don't need a liability hanging around me and getting in the way! When does he arrive?" There was an uneasy pause.

Rocke stood up again and looked through the window of Bell's office and saw a man with his feet up on the desk in his office, opposite that of Bell. He didn't know who he was, but he was wearing a smart, tight-fitting suit, with drainpipe trousers, and a pair of new winkle-pickers on his feet! Hoping his intuition is wrong, Rocke stormed out of Bell's office, through a room full of watching policemen, and shouted at the interloper.

"Hey you," he bellowed, "who the hell do you think you are, putting your feet up on my desk? Whoever you are, get out of my office!" Rocke walked into his office in a rage intent on expelling this man. The young man quickly stood up and smartened himself, straightened his tie and prepared to meet his new boss. His hair, Brylcreemed back in a DA, did not impress Rocke.

"Sorry sir," said the man, "I'm Detective Constable Warwick. I believe I'm going to be working with you?" Rocke was stopped in his tracks by the realisation of who was in front of him! His Liverpool accent became stronger when he was angry!

"God help me!" he said, throwing his hands in the air. "First thing you can do, Constable, is learn that you never put your feet on my desk, and learn some respect. If, and I repeat, if, we are going to be working together, then you are going to have to learn some rules." Warwick went to speak but didn't get the chance. "I don't care about your reputation," he shouted, with everyone in the outer office looking on.

"You do what I say when I say it, or I'm sending you back to London! Do I make myself clear?"

Warwick was like a deer startled in the headlights and stood motionless. The two stared at each other in silence, nose to nose, eyeball to eyeball, Warwick able to feel his boss's breath in his face. This stand-off was only broken by Bell calling Rocke from the other side of the office to go back to see him.

"Rocke - my office, now!" Rocke instructed Warwick to follow him, and they marched back through the open office, Warwick walking sheepishly behind his new boss, and entered Bell's office where he had obviously just received bad news.

"Just had a report of a nurse found dead in the alley behind the houses on Selborne Street," Bell informed Rocke. "Get up there now and take Warwick with you. You better explain where Selborne Street is, as we don't want another diplomatic incident!"

Bell and Rocke looked at Warwick, who was standing there slightly bemused. As Rocke exited the office, he muttered under his breath in the earshot of Bell.

"Sometimes I think you do this to me on purpose, or is it just that God hates me?" Bell couldn't help but smile as he watched Rocke walk out of his office. "Come on Warwick," Rocke said, "work to do, and only speak when you're spoken to! You got that?" Warwick nodded - he is too afraid to speak! They both grabbed their trench coats, and Rocke picked up his dark grey fedora, straightened it, and they headed out of Police Headquarters towards Rocke's car.

Chapter 3

Colour Blind

Rocke and Warwick walked out of the building onto Hope Street, opposite the Liverpool Philharmonic Hall. Rocke needed to establish some connection with Warwick, against his better judgment.

"Come on then Warwick: we need to talk on the way."

Warwick followed his boss out, and all of that inherent arrogance returned now that he was out of sight of the Chief.

"Talk about what?" he said in a thick London accent, shrugging his shoulders as if nothing needed to be said. Rocke was unimpressed by Warwick's apparent cockiness.

"There are some things you need to know about where we are going." Again, as if he had no cares in the world, Warwick responded to his boss.

"It's only Liverpool; it's not like being on the Flying Squad in London!"

As if Warwick had given Rocke another reason to hate him, the boss responded to this latest jibe.

"Actually Warwick," Rocke said emphatically, "Liverpool's Flying Squad, the Special Section, was set up a year before London's, so stop trying to be smart and know your police history! There is more to life than London - the world doesn't revolve around the capital!"

For once, Warwick was speechless! He put his head down and walked behind his boss, Realising that he couldn't say anything to make things better. They crossed over the road alongside the Philharmonic Hall. He decided, foolishly, to break the silence.

"What's this horrible building, then?" he said, pointing at the Hall.

"That," says Rocke proudly, "is one of the finest buildings of its type! This is the Philharmonic Hall, where just two years ago, I went to see Buddy Holly! What a night." A smile broke across his face as he remembered the night.

Rocke was suddenly going up in Warwick's estimation. "You saw Buddy Holly?" he said, a hint of incredulity in his voice. "You saw Buddy, in Liverpool?"

"Oh yes, London hasn't got everything you know!" replied Rocke sarcastically, "Buddy Holly and the Crickets, 20th March 1958! We've got some great groups up here you know."

Suddenly realising they were not socialising yet, Rocke became serious again.

"Anyway, enough about music, we need to have a chat." They walked to the car, a Ford Zodiac Mark 2 1956 model, two-tone colour with sky blue on top and dark grey at the bottom. It had white-walled tyres, and obviously wasn't the car Warwick was expecting.

"This is your car?" Warwick said with a note of surprise.

"No," Rocke responded sarcastically, "I'm nicking it, Warwick."

Warwick wasn't sure how to take that as he wasn't used to Liverpool humour yet.   "But   no, erm..............nicking ....I, er..." and then he muttered beneath his breath, "What does that even mean?"

Rocke unlocked the car and smirked to himself. As Warwick climbed into the car, he had a good look around. They turned left and headed up Hope Street towards the Anglican Cathedral. Warwick was amazed by the size of the cathedral that was still under construction.

"Wow, what is that?" Warwick was certainly impressed.

"That, Warwick," Rocke said proudly, "is our Cathedral - going to be one of the biggest in Europe they reckon! Anyway, we will do the tour later because we aren't going very far. When we get to the end of this road, we are on Upper Parliament Street. This road is the unofficial borderline between black and white Liverpool."

"What do you mean?" Warwick enquired. Rocke realised he needed to explain a bit more about his city to this Londoner in exile.

"There is historically a large black population in Liverpool and most of them live within this area here known Toxteth, though it is split into several areas, each of which has its own identity," he explained to his associate.

"Looks pretty grim to me," observed Warwick. Rocke continued as if Warwick hadn't uttered a word.

"Which is also where I grew up!" Warwick knew he had put his foot in it again! Rocke smirked to himself. "This used to be King John's hunting grounds in the 13th century you know," Rocke said to a slightly bemused Warwick.

"Hunting grounds? So what?" he responded.

"Well," said Rocke, "some of the locals still think it is!" Rocke chuckled to himself at his own joke.

The master of poor timing, Warwick decided to put his foot in his mouth again.

"I assume you've got a problem with the nig..... er...coloureds?" he spluttered. "So have we," he explained, answering his own question. "Scum the lot of them," Warwick proclaimed, "and everyone a thief! Should just lock them all up!" He was quite proud of himself. His boss had the exact opposite feeling.

"So that's your problem is it Warwick?" snapped Rocke. "The ignorance of youth. You know nothing, and views like that will see you sent back to where you came from - without a job! Keep your prejudice to yourself and only speak if you've got something to contribute!"

Rocke was rapidly losing his patience with Warwick, and he didn't think much of him to start with. Warwick just grunted to himself and didn't see the point in talking. The car turned right into Princes Road and passed the Synagogue, then left into Selborne Street and pulled up next to the parked police car. Rocke and Warwick exited the car and walked towards the constable on duty.

Chapter 4

A Pretty Nurse

Rocke walked over to the policeman, who quickly stood to attention, recognising his approaching superior officer.

"Hello sir," he said promptly, "follow me."

Rocke and Warwick followed the PC to the alley behind the houses on Selborne Street to where John McKenzie, the Police Surgeon, was kneeling over the body of a woman. The alley was dark, and damp, and had an almost overpowering smell of rotting food. They stepped carefully around the dog muck on the floor, broken bottles, cigarette butts and other rubbish. Rocke walked over to McKenzie, who was obviously a well-known colleague, a portly, stocky Scotsman in his mid-fifties, with a white beard and balding spot on the top of his head.

"Hi George," McKenzie said in his quiet Glaswegian accent. "Another nice one for you here."

Rocke looked down at the body of the dead woman. Her face was ashen, and her eyes were staring right into Rocke's. Her blonde hair was a mess, and her nurse's uniform was ripped across the breast and thighs. Her handbag was near to the body, and she had one shoe next to her, with the other about twenty yards further down the alley. Warwick's cockiness was knocked out of him as he stared at the body, almost in a trance.

"What d'ya reckon John?" Rocke asked McKenzie, obviously unphased at the sight of a dead body, unlike his young compatriot. McKenzie stood up to talk to Rocke. McKenzie immediately went into his professional mode, ready to give his report.

"Young nurse, early twenties." McKenzie suddenly spotted a face he didn't recognise. "Who's the new boy?" he enquired of Rocke.

"Sorry John, this is DC Warwick, another brat with a big gob they've sent me - this one is from the Mighty Met," he said, pretending to be impressed. Warwick went to shake hands, but McKenzie's hands were still dirty and stained from the examination, so Warwick quickly withdrew his hand. Rocke turned to Warwick to continue the introduction.

"Warwick, McKenzie is our most experienced Police Surgeon, so watch, listen and learn."

Looking to have some fun with the new boy, McKenzie joined in the fun.

"You calling me old?" he exclaimed to Rocke, but Warwick just muttered under his breath, while fetching his notebook from his jacket pocket.

"You're both old to me." Rocke blanked Warwick and returned to McKenzie and got down to business.

"What happened to her?" McKenzie knelt again by the body, and Rocke crouched down alongside him. McKenzie pointed to the wounds as he described the attack.

"Well, as you can see, there was a blow to the back of the head behind the right ear," he said, as he carefully lifted the victim's head, "probably from that piece of wood," as he pointed to a block of wood nearby, which clearly had blood on it. "However," he added, "she has been strangled. She has severe bruising, probably caused by the fall against the wall and then onto the ground. I will tell you more after the post mortem. If you look at the throat, she was strangled with a thin ligature, which is probably what killed her, not the impact of the fall or the blow to the head."

Rocke carefully pondered on everything that he had heard, and inevitably had questions for his colleague.

"Uniform is ripped, John: any sign of sexual assault?" McKenzie was happy to answer his question.

"There is nothing yet to indicate any sexual assault at this stage, though there is a bit of reddening at the top of her thigh, so that might develop. She has had intercourse recently but no obvious signs of rape."

Rocke was relieved, but still reserving judgement at this early stage. Warwick decided to ask a question and maybe repair some of the damage.

"When did she die, Doc?" McKenzie and Rocke looked up at him in unison, and McKenzie was happy to acknowledge Warwick's question.

"A sensible question, Warwick. She was probably killed somewhere between midnight and three o'clock. However, I can tell you more when I've done the p.m., which I will get done as quickly as possible." Rocke had seen and heard enough.

"Thanks, John. Anything else we need to know at this stage?" McKenzie did have more information for him.

"See what you make of this: over by the wall, we found these." McKenzie held out his hand to show two silver coins. Rocke picked one up to examine it more closely. Rocke was surprised.

"Is that an American quarter?" he enquired.

"Certainly is, George." Warwick again wanted to contribute to the conversation.

"So why has she got US currency?" He was totally confused. Rocke wasn't, which puzzled Warwick.

"Interesting. Thanks, John. Is the photographer on the way?" Warwick felt like he now had a number of questions, but held back for now.

"Yes, the photographer should be here soon," McKenzie advised, "then we can move her. You happy with that?"

Rocke was happy to confirm. "Yes, those're good, thanks, John. OK Warwick, let's go and see if we can try to piece together what happened." Rocke and Warwick took a few steps back, and then Rocke started walking around, with his arms moving around as he thought out loud.

"She came into the entry, and ...."

"Into what?" Warwick asked with a confused expression on his face. Rocke was nonplussed at first.

"What?" Warwick tried to restate his query. "You said into the entry....... Entry to what?"

Rocke realised there was a language barrier here.

"No," he explained, "entry - entry, alley, where we are now." Obviously not happy with having to explain himself. "Didn't realise I had to translate as well!" He got his train of thought back and tried to visualise the crime. "Her shoe came off a couple of yards down the," and with real emphasis, "ALLEY, and if she was struck from behind, she wouldn't have had time to see her attacker."

As Rocke talked it through, he was following the actions with his hands and muttering to himself in the process. Warwick watched and made notes as he observed.

"She gets knocked down, but not unconscious. Handbag is still here so it wasn't robbery: no obvious signs of sexual assault either, so what is the motive? Strangling to me is more of a reactive than a premeditated action, and maybe personal." Warwick looked up from his notebook and wanted to impress his new boss.

"She knew her attacker?" he asked Rocke.

"I think so," Rocke agreed. "American currency too. But what was she doing here?" At this point, he stopped in his tracks, and again Warwick felt the need to ask his boss to explain.

"What do you mean?" he asked.

"This is the black part of Toxteth, Warwick," he responded, though without the sarcasm this time, "this whole area around Granby Street and Upper Parliament Street is mainly inhabited by the people of Caribbean and African descent, not the whites."

"And you think some nigger did it?" Warwick couldn't help himself speaking, when he should have stayed silent.

Rocke grabbed Warwick by the collar of his coat and pinned him against the wall in anger. Warwick was shocked and speechless.

"If you ever use that word again," Rocke screamed, "I will have you thrown out of the force! You will respect everybody whatever the colour of their skin or way they speak. You are a foreigner in this city - so don't ever let me catch you using that word again. Do you hear me?" Rocke was almost foaming at the mouth, his face red with rage and his eyes on fire. Warwick had to apologise, and quickly.

"OK, OK I'm sorry Guv, Blimey; I didn't mean nothing by it," he blurted out in his strongest cockney accent. He was genuinely scared. It did nothing to calm his boss down.

"But you still said it! You still said it. That tongue will get you in trouble here, and not just with me with. Use that word in the wrong company and I won't be able to save you. Do you hear me?" Warwick nodded in agreement.

Rocke let go of Warwick, who then straightened his own tie and pulled himself together. McKenzie had observed the altercation and could see that Warwick was in shock, and wasn't sure if he needed to intervene, but now headed back towards the body and carried on as if nothing has happened. Warwick was sheepish and kept his head down. They carried on with the investigation.

"Constable Higgins, who found the body?" Rocke asked of the watching constable. He took his notebook out and gave the detective the information he needed.

"It was a lady, Mrs. Mimba," he said as he stumbled over the name.   Warwick foolishly laughed, which lead to him receiving an evil look from his boss. The constable continued.

"Erm, Mrs. Mimba McLaughlin who lives in the bottom flat at 35, Selborne Street - this is her back gate" he indicated, pointing at the gate they were standing by. "She opened the gate and almost walked on the dead body! She is in shock, but she is in the house and has a friend sitting with her." He finalised his report and put the notebook back into the breast pocket of his uniform.

"OK, thanks, Higgins," Rocke said, looking for some more information. "What was found with the body? Any personal effects apart from the handbag?"

"No, just the handbag, sir," Higgins responded promptly. Rocke and Warwick went to the discarded handbag and crouched down to examine it. The detective opened the small black leather handbag, and took out the items one by one, examining each item carefully. The i.d. card was first, which Rocke examined closely.

He started to automatically read out what he was seeing.

"Nurse Helen Smith, from the Southern Hospital'," he said and then turned to Warwick to explain further. "That's on the corner of Hill Street and Caryl Street - spelt C.A.R.Y.L. but pronounced Carl. We've also got," indicating to Warwick that he needs to write this down: "A hair brush, small bottle of perfume, lipstick, compact, latch key, black notebook." This item was of great interest and placed at one side. Rocke then took out the purse and opened it to see that it still had money in it. "No money was taken, so probably not a robbery." Warwick aimed to get back into his boss' good books.

"Enough money for a taxi home, sir," he interjected, "and some spare change too."

Rocke opened the small black notebook to see if there were any clues to help them. "It looks like a diary," he advised his colleague.

"What does it say for today?" Warwick enquired. Their hopes were dashed, and Rocke was exasperated.

"Nothing! Yesterday says PB, and a couple of days ago the same, and previous weeks we keep seeing PB. We need to find out who PB is," he said to Warwick, who made a note in his book of the initials. "There is also a note," he continued, "she has a couple of weeks ago saying 'have got to tell him no! Too intense, too much.' Is 'him' this PB, or is PB a regular appointment and not connected?" he said, though more as a rhetorical question thinking out loud.

"She doesn't say much about anything, really, does she?" Warwick offered. Rocke quickly concurred.

"I would suggest this is not her main diary. Probably uses it for recording thoughts, or reminders, but felt she had to write it down. Oh well, it gives us something and hopefully, the main diary will tell us more."

Rocke closed the diary and called over to the PC again.

"You stay here, Higgins," he said, with a warning, "and keep your eyes open. We will talk to the neighbour first, and then she can get on with her day. Warwick, come with me and keep your gob shut unless you have something sensible to contribute!"

Warwick mouthed 'gob' as he didn't know what it meant. Rocke smiled knowingly at McKenzie, who was still kneeling by the body, as Warwick trudged down the alley towards their car. He had shown Warwick, who was the boss, and McKenzie knew it. They walked around to visit Mrs. McLaughlin.

Rocke knew he had to keep a watchful eye on his new assistant because now they were dealing with the public.

"Right Warwick," he instructed, pointing his finger at him, "if you want to survive more than one day in this city, you have to learn some important points. Liverpool has been built on the back of a strong, multi-cultural mix, but you have to know about the underlying tensions in the area between the blacks and the whites. The black people don't come into the city centre because they get monkey chants and racial insults, so they stay in their own area, which is in this small part of Toxteth around Upper Parliament Street, Princes Road and Granby Street. To some people, we are the enemy here: we are the 'J's', they are the 'shines'." Warwick, not for the first-time today, was confused.

"What's that all about then?" he asked looking puzzled.

"The local whites decided to call them the 'shines' because their dark skin shines!" He then added sarcastically, "How clever is that?"

Warwick started to chuckle until he caught the evil eye from Rocke.

"Because we called them the 'shines'," he added, "they called us the 'J's', the John Bull's, the symbol of imperialist Britain!" Warwick was indignant.

"But this is our country; we were here first!" he said emphatically. "Why should we be kowtowing to them - they should go back to where they came from!"

Rocke was livid.

"Listen, Warwick, some of these families have been here for 150 years or more, so they are as British as you and me. You need to lose the attitude, do you understand me?" For some unknown reason, Warwick became more confident and able to hold his own, or so he thought. However, he felt he had to acquiesce at this point.

"Whatever makes you happy, Guv," he said, knowing they were the words he had to utter.

They arrived at Mrs. McLaughlin's house in an uneasy silence. It was a beautiful Georgian terraced house of which she had the ground floor. Rocke knocked on the door and waited for an answer. Mrs. McLaughlin, still obviously distressed, answered the door nervously.

"Hello?" she said with a tremble to her voice. She was a lady of African origin who had grown up in Liverpool, and lived on her own, now that her children had grown up and her husband had died a few years ago. She was about 75 years old, by the look of her, thought Rocke.

"Hello, Mrs. McLaughlin. My name is Detective Inspector Rocke. I wonder if I could come in and talk to you about what happened this morning?"

He showed her his identification card to reassure her. Mrs. McLaughlin showed them into her front room, which was obviously kept especially for visitors. There were an old but tidy horsehair couch and armchair, and a coal fire in the fireplace, surrounded by a dark wood mantelpiece. She had family photos on the walls, and heavy curtains at the window looking out over Selborne Street. There was an ornate coffee table on top of the rug in the middle of the room, and a china teapot with two cups on the table. Her friend, of about the same age, was sitting in the armchair.

She kindly welcomed them into the room.

"Come in and sit down sir, please," she said in a gentle voice, with a strong African lilt in her accent.

"Oh thank you, Mrs. McLaughlin," Rocke said respectfully, "please sit down too. We won't keep you long." Rocke sat down but indicated to Warwick that he should stand by the wall behind him. He began the questioning as gently as he felt he could do in the circumstances.

"I know this has been a big shock to you, and I don't want to make things worse, but I need to ask you some questions." She nodded in agreement. "Did you hear anything last night?" he asked. "Any disturbance; unusual noises?"

She talked in such a quiet voice that the policemen strain to hear her.

"I'm sorry, but my hearing ain't good no more, so I don't hear a ting. First, I know is when I opens my gate and nearly walk on the poor lady." She starts to cry again, but at the same time tries to retain her composure. Rocke has to continue the questioning but does so respectfully.

"Did you recognise the lady? Have you seen her before?" After a quick, deep breath, she answered his question.

"I think so. She looks like the girl that Gus brought back to the house a few times recently. He always says hello to me, lovely man."

Warwick butted in before his boss could ask the next question, which at first, Rocke was annoyed at.

"Erm, Mrs. McLaughlin, who is Gus? Does he live local?" It was an intelligent question, which she was happy to answer, though Mrs. McLaughlin replied to Rocke, not Warwick.

"Oh, he's a lovely boy, Gus," she says warmly. "Plays with the Caribbean Steel Band at that club in town, but I don't know what is called. He lives in the flat upstairs, but I don't think he came back last night."

She suddenly realised the significance of what she had said, saw the faces of the policemen, and panicked.

"Oh please, please, he is a lovely boy and wouldn't hurt a fly." She was now getting agitated. "He couldn't have done something like that, he really liked her."

Rocke immediately looked to reassure her.

"That's alright Mrs. McLaughlin; we would have found out that kind of information anyway, so don't worry. It doesn't mean anything at all; we just need to speak to him. Is he usually around during the day?" She was quick to answer and felt happier to comment further.

"He goes to the club in the afternoon and then plays until the early morning," she said, "so he sleeps till dinnertime." Having had time to think, Rocke took a guess at the club.

"Is it the Jacaranda Club where he plays?" With a sudden realisation, Mrs. McLaughlin answered brightly.

"Yes, yes, that's the one. Lovely boy." She was now more relaxed then suddenly remembered her manners. "Oh, would you gentlemen like a cup of tea?" She made a move to stand up, but her questioning was nearly over anyway. He stood to leave, indicating to Warwick that they were done.

"Thank you, Mrs. McLaughlin, we will leave you in peace for now. Try not to worry - we will make sure that one of our constables keeps an extra eye on the area so you don't have to worry about anything." He replaced his hat while doffing it slightly to say thank you. Mrs. McLoughlin was clearly happy that the ordeal was over.

"Oh thank you, thank you, sir." She led them to the front door and waved them off as they headed back towards their car.

Chapter Five

The Jac

Rocke started the car, as he and Warwick headed back into town towards the Jacaranda Club. Warwick checked his notebook as he asked where they were going.

"So how did you know it was the, erm, Jacaranda Club that Mrs. McLoughlin was talking about?" His boss was happy to inform him.

"Simple, Warwick. The only black faces you will see in the town centre are the musicians of the Caribbean Steel Band that play at the Jacaranda, also a well-known hangout for nurses. It seems like the best place to start to me." Warwick agreed and was starting to be impressed by his new boss.

"So now we are on the way to speak to its owner, Allan Williams," he continued, "who also has the Wyvern Club, one of the few clubs in town where you can get a proper drink! Know your city, Warwick."

However, in a split second, he was back to being the ignorant bigot Rocke has perceived him to be.

"Sorry for laughing at that woman's name, but what kind of name is Mimba?" Warwick chuckled again to himself. He was not expecting much of a response and was surprised at what he was about to hear.

"It is a slave name from the Akan region of Ghana," he explained. "It would have been passed down through the family, and the McLaughlin, as you will have noticed from the photographs in her house, was from her white husband, who is most likely a Scot: there are a lot of Scots in Liverpool, as well as Irish, Welsh, Italians, Germans and many more nationalities, and lots of mixed marriages."

Rocke was becoming tired of having to hand-hold this ignorant young detective. Warwick, however, was, not for the first time, quietly impressed, but wouldn't say so. He did, as ever, have a comment to make.

"But come on Guv, marrying outside of your culture - it doesn't make sense! What have they got in common? White people made the coloured people slaves, so why mix? Then you have to think about the half-caste kids they have. It's not fair on them! We had one half-caste kid in our class at school, and he didn't know which tribe to be in."

Rocke slammed on the brakes suddenly, nearly throwing Warwick through the windscreen! He was angry and shouted at his boss.

"Blimey Guv," he screamed in his strongest cockney accent, "what the hell are you doing?" His boss turned to his sidekick and felt like punching him there and then. He restrained himself before delivering a broadside blast at his passenger.

"Don't speak about what you don't know and don't understand! You have no idea what that poor woman has had to go through, so don't judge her or her choices. I mean it Warwick, shape up or ship out because unless you change your attitude, we are going to fall out and, trust me; you don't want that to happen because your career will be over! Mrs. McLaughlin is actually more English than I am! My father came to Liverpool from Holland and married an Irish-Liverpool girl. Does that make me half-caste or is it just a colour prejudice?" Warwick finally was feeling ashamed as his face turned the colour of a blushing strawberry.

"I'm sorry Guv, I, I," he stuttered, "I didn't think." Rocke was quick with his riposte.

"Exactly, that's your problem. Now learn to put your brain into gear before you open your gob! Can we get on with the case, please, as we have a killer to catch?" Warwick wisely decided to change the subject.

"Well, if you ask me, Gus sounds like the one to go after." Warwick counted on his fingers as he made his points.

"It was his on/ off girlfriend; he didn't come home, and the body was found at the back of the house where he lives. And now he is on the run!" Although his boss was impressed, he needed to dampen his enthusiasm.

"Don't jump to conclusions, Warwick. He is our number-one suspect, of course, but the trail has just started. Don't forget the US currency." Rocke turned right and towards Liverpool's Chinatown on the left, in the shadow of the unfinished Cathedral on the right. The education needed to continue.

"One of our many ethnic populations is based in Chinatown. The oldest Chinese community in Europe was established in Liverpool in the early 19th century you know Warwick," he said, smiling at his companion. "And they do great food too!" of "our many ethnic populations is based in Chinatown. The oldest Chinese community in Europe was established in Liverpool in the early 19th century you know Warwick," he said, smiling at his companion. "And they do great food too!"

Warwick smiled for the first time! They turn left down Seel Street in front of the Wyvern Club. "That's Williams' other club, The Wyvern. However, it is his coffee club that we are interested in." They pulled up opposite the Jacaranda in Slater Street and parked outside an art shop.

The Jacaranda was a small coffee club in Slater Street, which overlooked the street. It had a coffee bar on the ground floor, with tables and chairs as you walked in. However, at this time of the morning, the door was locked. Rocke peered through the dirty glass, and they spotted a cleaner, so he banged at the door. The cleaning lady, a stocky woman in her 50s, had her hair tied up in a scarf and had a cigarette hanging from her bottom lip. She walked over to the door and shouted through to her visitors.

"Sorry love," she shouted in a strong Irish accent, "we're not open yet. Come back later." Her visitors weren't ready to leave though.

"Is the owner here?" enquired Warwick.

"Who wants to know?" she shouted back, a lot louder than she needed to. Warwick put his warrant card to the window and answered sarcastically in his best, London accent.

"Police, Mrs."

Rocke interrupted him as he saw the reaction on the cleaner's face. They had a conversation through the glass.

"Local police, mum," he said, "just need to speak to the owner." She was happy to talk to him.

"Sorry luv," she answered politely, "he's not in yet, just one of the band." This piqued his interest immediately.

"Which of the band is it?" he asked in hope that it would be Gus. She thought for a moment:

"Sammy I think, son; he's downstairs." Okay, thought Rocke, he would do for a start.

"Mum?" said Warwick. "Is that your mum?"

"What are you talking about?"

"But you called her mum, and she called you son?"

Rocke just glared at his sidekick, shaking his head in despair, before turning back to speak to the lady.

"Can you open the door for us, so we can speak to him?" he asked. Rocke turned to his colleague as the door is unlocked.

"Did you get a refund then, Warwick," who was even more bemused?

"Where from Guv?"

"The charm school!" was his swift retort.

Rocke smiled to himself - Warwick wasn't impressed! The cleaner opened the door and let them go in. The chairs were on the tables and there was a pile of dirt in the middle of the floor where she had been sweeping.

"What's your name love?" Warwick enquired. However, this immediately put her on the defensive.

"Why do you want to know?" she asked him, a scowl coming over her face as she stood there, a formidable woman with her hands on her hips. Warwick was riled by this and responded arrogantly.

"Just answer the question, lady." She snarled Warwick and Rocke stepped in yet again.

"Just to be polite, save calling you Mrs. or 'Luv'," he said. It has the desired effect.

"Well, my name is Mabel. Mabel Thornton, 28 Essex Street, The Dingle." She then turned to Warwick, sarcastically; "Need to know what I had for breakfast son?" Warwick was embarrassed and Rocke smiled, as she gave Rocke a wink.

"Thanks, Mabel, is Sammy down that way?"

He pointed to the stairway at the rear of the club, and Mabel nodded in agreement. The two officers walked down the stairs decorated with artwork from the students from the local art college. They appeared at the basement which was dimly lit. There was a bar on the right with a coffee machine, teapots and bottles of Pepsi. At the far end was a small stage, only a couple of inches from the ground, covered in torn, worn-out carpet. The walls were decorated with an exotic looking mural painted by the art students who also frequent the Jac, as it was commonly referred to. On the stage was a set of steel pans, and the musician, presumed to be Sammy, tapping away, oblivious to his guests.

Rocke coughed to get his attention.

"Erm, are you Sammy?" Sammy, a Trinidadian in his late 20s, replies without looking up, in a strong West-Indian accent.

"Who wants to know?" Warwick was about to speak but decided against it after a glare from his superior.

"My name is Rocke; I'm a policeman." Sammy jumped up with a start and secreted a joint of marijuana in one of the steel pans.

"Sorry sir, just tending to me pans." They pretended as if nobody had noticed the joint.

"Sorry to disturb you, I was looking for Gus." Sammy, carefully choosing every word, answered the policeman.

"You won't see him for a while yet, too early. I'm the arranger and pan maker; I do the repairs and tune-ups, so I'm always in early. What's he done?" Rocke ignored the question and carried on with his own enquiries.

"Do you know his girlfriend?" he said. Warwick observed and took notes.

"Helen? Yeah, I know her, though she was and wasn't his girl, know what I mean?" He chuckled to himself. "Sometimes together, sometimes not. Nice girl. She OK?"

Again, Rocke ignored the question.

"Were they OK last night?" Both policemen were keen to know the answer.

"Oh," he laughs again, "day had a big row! Some Yank swaggers in thinking he owns the place and is all over Helen," at which point, Warwick interrupted.

"A Yank? In here?" His voice was both bemused and surprised. Warwick gave a look towards Rocke as the coins found by Helen's body could make sense. Sammy, virtually ignoring Warwick's response, continued.

"Yeah, one of them US servicemen. Gus was really angry! They have a shouting match in the bar, and Helen storms out; I see it with my own eyes. Gus had words outside, and she went home in a taxi." Now it was starting to get interesting.

"Did Gus follow her?" he enquired.

"No," replied Sammy, "he came back down here and kicked one of the pans - that's what I'm fixing now!"

Sammy suddenly realised something was wrong and became more cagey with his answers.

"How soon after did he leave?" Rocke continued. Sammy was not happy.

"Hey, what's going on man, is something wrong?" Sammy looked worried as his interrogation continued.

"We just need to talk to Gus; that's all," he was told politely, Warwick looking to capture every nuance of Sammy's responses.

"Something happen to Helen?" he asked, but his inquisitor was giving nothing away yet.

"Did you leave with Gus last night?" At this point, Sammy decided he should say no more.

"I don't like these questions" he explained, gesturing with his hands for the conversation to be stopped. Warwick jumped in with both feet without thinking about the consequences.

"A woman is dead and we don't have time for nonsense, Sammy boy, so tell us what....."

"Who you calling 'boy'?" At the mention of the word, 'boy' Sammy went mad. Rocke became angry with Warwick and snapped at him.

"Warwick, upstairs and wait for me, now!"

Warwick stomped upstairs in disbelief pleading his innocence as an embarrassed Rocke apologised for his colleague.

"Please forgive his ignorance, he has just come up from London, and you know what they're like down there!" In fact, Sammy was all too familiar with life in the capital.

"That I do, sir" he concurred, "I was in London for three years, as was Gus. Did your 'boy'," and he emphasised the word, specifically, "say Helen is dead?" Rocke confirmed that fact for him.

"I'm afraid so," he advised, "she was found in the entry behind his flat this morning." Sammy quickly realised what was happening.

"And you think Gus did it?" he said in disbelief. "No way, man, no way," he said, shaking his head.

"We aren't accusing anyone," he was assured, "just starting to work out what happened, so we just need to talk to him."

Sammy decided he had to make amends for his earlier comments.

"When I said he was angry," he laughed nervously, "it was nothing really; he was OK after kicking the pan." He smiled hopefully, but Rocke wasn't fooled by Sammy's change of story but was happy to let him carry on if needed.

"But none of us knows what happens when it is over a girl," his new policeman friend suggested. "Were they in love?"

"He might have been," added Sammy cautiously, "but she wasn't. It was casual, nothing serious, you know what I mean?" Rocke nodded in agreement but had to push on.

"What time did Gus go home?" he asked. Sammy thought for a moment before answering.

"We usually go home together, unless we get lucky if you know what I mean?" he laughed with a mischievous chuckle.

"I think I get the idea," said Rocke laughing. "Did you go home together last night?" Sammy continued to laugh to himself and then looked up at his questioner.

"No sir," he smiled, "I got lucky!"

Rocke smiled knowingly.

"Lucky man, Sammy!" he said, "Gus didn't go home last night either. Did he get lucky?" Sammy stopped smiling.

"No," he replied, "he left on his own."

"And he didn't go home?" Sammy looked worried. "No."

"Anywhere else he would go?" He pondered for a moment and then replied.

"Only my flat," he suggested, "but I wasn't there."

"Does he have a key to your flat?" he enquired. Sammy knew he had to answer, and maybe this could help his friend.

"Yes, there's a spare under the mat. Maybe he is there," he said hopefully. He knew what question was coming next.

"And where is your flat?" Sammy had no alternative but to answer correctly.

"I live at 47, Selborne Street, flat 2." Rocke looked surprised and pleased at once.

"Just up from Gus?" he asked.

"Yes, that's right sir," Sammy concurred. Without knowing, Sammy had just implicated himself.

"Where were you last night?" Sammy was asked, which sent him into a panic.

"Am I a suspect too?" he asked, his voice wavering as he spoke. "Hey man, I'm just trying to help; I don't know what happened."

"We just need to eliminate everyone from the enquiry," he was advised. "I'm going to need the name and address of that lucky lady you were with last night, too." Sammy was reluctant, but again, knew he had no choice.

"She's going to love me," he said laughing with embarrassment, "it's nothing serious you know?"

Rocke was happy to reassure him. "We will keep it quiet, don't worry." Sammy, reluctantly, revealed the name of his conquest.

"Her name is Dorothy. Dot Collinson, she's a friend of Helen's from the hospital - they share a flat. She will be in work now. Oh my God," he suddenly panicked, "she won't know about Helen! You'll have to tell her easily." He had nothing to worry about.

"We will; don't worry. Which hospital does she work in?" Sammy stumbled over his words as he started to understand the implications of what had happened.

"The Southern. Can't believe it, poor Helen. But Gus won't have done it, no way, sir, no way, no way," he kept muttering as his words dropped off into the basement air.

"Your loyalty does you credit," he was assured, "and we're not accusing.."

"No, you don't know Gus," he pleaded. "He's a pacifist! He's a vegetarian too - won't eat meat because the animals get killed!" He felt he had done enough, but the questions kept coming.

"Did you see who he was arguing with, apart from Helen?" Sammy was happy to answer these questions now.

"Oh yes," he said proudly, "some damn Yank from that air force base! Three of them always in here, shooting their damn stupid mouths off and trying to get our girls. He was putting his arm around Helen trying to wind up Gus. Helen was having none of it, so they start shouting and Helen walks out, followed by Gus and the Yank. Some argument outside, and Helen and the Yank get into the taxi, not Gus, so if you want to know who killed her, I'd look at that Yank!"

Sammy felt he had made the case in defence of his friend.

"Thank you, Sammy, I appreciate your help," said Rocke. "If Gus comes down here, just ask him to call Detective Inspector Rocke at Police HQ." Sammy took the card handed to him.

"Yes, yes, sure man, OK man, will if I see him." Sammy gratefully returned to his pans, and he picked up the remains of his joint, as Rocke headed up the stairs again. With one long drag on the joint, Sammy sat down and pondered over everything that had just happened.

Chapter Six

Our Friend Sammy

As Rocke got to the top of the stairs, he saw Warwick and the cleaner chatting away. He was pleasantly surprised.

"Oh, Mr. Rocky," she giggled, mispronouncing his name by mistake, "this is such a charming boy, even though he is a cockney!" Warwick sat there with a grin on his face after the previous quip from his boss!

"Charming?" said Rocke with surprise, "is he indeed? I never knew that!" Warwick decided to make the most of his new friendship.

"Well," Warwick told his boss, "Mabel was telling me how last night, her friend Mavis........"

"Mavis told me that there was this argument," Mabel explained as she interrupted Warwick, talking, like most Liverpool ladies, with her hands, "started by one of them art students who were sitting over here. He said to that poor girl 'Nice to see you with your clothes on!' Ooh," she cried making both men jump, "I mean, how rude? Not appropriate at all." She was finished, at least they thought she was.

Rocke decided to jump in. "And do you know which..."

"The student was one of them layabouts who are always hanging around here," as he was quickly interrupted by Mabel again, "bumming cups of tea and butties, trying to get some money together. He plays with a group sometimes here - his name is John something, up at the art school." Warwick added a quick comment.

"And Mavis also saw the argument..."

"Ooh," she yelled again, "yes, what an argument it was with poor Gus, his girl and this American gentleman, well, I say gentleman, but they are anything but! Always coming in here thinking they own the place! It's not like in the war - they were charming back then, with their smart uniforms, great music, oh how charming, bringing us stockings and...." Rocke interrupted this nostalgic journey with a cough.

"Ahem! Thanks, Mabel, Sammy was telling me the same thing about the American. When does this John normally come in?"

She sat bolt upright again.

"Not in the morning that's for sure! Always last to leave, and often gets a lift with one of the staff so he doesn't have to pay for the taxi! Bum - nothing good will come of him; that's for sure!" She continued to shake her head even though she'd finished talking.

"Thank you, Mabel," said Warwick, "you've been so helpful. Sorry, I can't stop longer, but we need to get on." Mabel grabbed him by the arm, lovingly, thinking she has found a new boy to mother.

"My pleasure Paul - see you again I hope."

Rocke was watching on in disbelief! Had he misjudged his new colleague? They exited the Jacaranda and climbed back into the car. They sat in the car and talked briefly to catch up.

"Stupid old gossip," Warwick opined dismissively, "you can get anything from them old ladies if you smarm them!" He thought he was really clever: his boss was so disappointed.

"And there was me thinking you'd made progress!" he said with a sigh. "Too good to be true I suppose."

Warwick was non-plussed. Rocke knew they needed to make progress with the investigation.

"Right," he said, changing the subject, "our friend Sammy lives a couple of doors away from Gus, and Gus sometimes crashes at his flat. So that should be our first stop. Helen worked at the Southern Hospital with a girl called Dot that Sammy was with last night. All good friends!"

Warwick, however, thought they should be looking elsewhere.

"But what about this Yank?" he demanded. "Where the hell is he from? What's he doing in a little place like Liverpool?" Again, he had managed to annoy his boss.

"The little town of Liverpool was the HQ of the battle of the Atlantic in World War 2, and one of the most heavily bombed cities across the country, for your information," he told his pupil, who was open-mouthed. "About twenty miles outside Liverpool is Burtonwood Air Force Base, which was commandeered during the war by the US Air Force. They are still here, and have thousands of servicemen cooped up on the base, and guess where they all like to party?" This was Warwick's chance to win a few brownie points back.

"In Liverpool?" he suggested cautiously.

"Exactly. We have to find an unnamed US serviceman on a US Air Force base, which is going to be damn hard - especially if he did it! It could be a logistical nightmare. Don't even know if we can get onto the base to start with! Anyway, first things first, let's get back to Selborne Street and see if we can find our missing musician."

They drove back up the hill by the cathedral and returned to Selborne Street, pulling up outside Sammy's house, which was only two doors away from Gus's house - where a constable was standing guard, as instructed.

Chapter Seven

I Haven't Done Nothing

The two detectives exited the car, and Rocke looked under the mat. There was no key, which in a way was a good thing he thought, but worth a shot. He knocked on the door and heard the footsteps of a lady walking towards them. A young black girl in her twenties opened the door and looked suspiciously at them.

"Hello love," he whispered, holding his finger to his lips, "my name is Rocke, and I'm a policeman, could you let me in quietly please?"

He showed her his card, and she opened the door without saying a word.

"Flat 2?" he mouthed, and she indicated that it was upstairs. They walked quietly up the stairs and located flat 2. Rocke knocked at the door and listened for any movement. There was no answer at first, but then a distant Trinidad accent is heard.

"Sammy, is that you?" the voice said, sounding scared.

The policemen didn't answer, hoping that the inhabitant would come to the door. Suddenly, there were footsteps walking towards the door. It slowly opened and Rocke and Warwick pushed the door, to see the frightened face of the man they presume to be Gus. He panicked and headed for the back room, chased swiftly by Warwick. There was nowhere to run, and by the time Rocke had entered the room, Warwick had Gus pinned against the wall.

Gus protested his innocence.

"I haven't done nothing, let me go," he cried, obviously scared.

"Then why run and hide, Gus?" Warwick shouted in his face. They were nose to nose now.

"I panicked," he protested, "when I saw the police in the alley this morning! What's going on?" Rocke decided to step in.

"What are you doing hiding yourself away in this flat for?" he enquired. "Warwick, let him sit down, but stand by the door, in case he changes his mind!"

Gus sat down in the armchair, and Warwick stared menacingly at him. Rocke pulled up a wooden chair from the table and sat in front of the suspect. Gus looked terrified.

"Do you know why the police are downstairs Gus?" he asked. He appeared to be clueless, but that could have been for show.

"No," he answered, "but I didn't want to go home, so I came to find Sammy, but he wasn't here, so I just stayed here." The questions continued.

"Why not go home, Gus? What are you afraid of?" He was shaking nervously and stumbled over his words.

"Just don't like the police, you know?" he shrugged.

Rocke decided he had to move the conversation on.

"We need to talk to you, Gus, because this morning, they found the body of Helen Smith in the entry behind your house?" Gus was visibly shocked and distraught. He stood up and Warwick blocked the door, but Gus just paced the room, rubbing his hands on his head in disbelief.

"What?" he exclaimed. "Helen dead? No, no, what is going on, no this can't be true, it can't be true?" He kept pacing the floor until Rocke could take no more.

"Sit done Gus!" he yelled, having the desired effect. "We just need to talk to you; nobody is accusing you of anything." He sat down again in the chair, biting his nails and still visibly distressed.

"Helen dead? I can't believe it. Who did it?" Gus looked to them for answers, when they wanted answers from him.

There was a pause before Gus realised what was happening.

"No," no," he protested, "I didn't do it! I couldn't hurt her; I love her" and then he realised what he was saying and had to change his phrase, sounding more melancholy: "I loved her." He bowed his head with genuine sadness, pausing for a moment. Rocke broke the silence.

"But you realise we have to talk to you about your relationship and what happened last night?" There was no response from Gus. "No one is accusing you of anything," he continued. Gus didn't respond to the statement but carried on his train of thought.

"Who would do this?" he asked rhetorically. He then answered himself. "It was that Yank!" he said decisively, standing up. "Him and his big mouth carried my Helen away in a taxi last night."

Rocke decided to go with the conversation, but use it to his advantage.

"So we've been told. Do you know his name?" Warwick had his pencil poised hoping for some useful information.

"Chuck something," he muttered, "Warsofski, Warshowski, something like that. You need to talk to him." As Warwick wrote it down, Rocke continued his questioning.

"OK that helps, and we will talk to him. Now, we know what happened at the Jac between you, Helen and this American. But what happened outside the Jac? You three had an argument?" Now they were getting to the important conversation that nobody overheard.

"I just kept asking Helen to stay with me," Gus explained, "but the Yank promised to look after her and protect her from me. She didn't want to go and told him to get away from her too, but he jumped into the taxi. She told him to get out, but he closed the door and that was the last I saw of her. She looked back at me as it pulled away, but I couldn't do nothing." Warwick chipped in with a question, without checking with his boss first, which didn't go down well. However, it was the natural next question.

"So you went back into the club?" Gus continued his story.

"Yes, the other Yanks were laughing at me, so I just went downstairs with Sammy, and I kicked the pans! What could I do?"

"So why hide out here?" Rocke asked him.

"I didn't want police asking questions!" he responded quickly.

"About what?" he was asked. Gus thought carefully about what he said next.

"I ran away from the police in London!" he said ashamedly. At the sound of London, Warwick's attention was piqued.

"What for?" Gus was obviously sharing this information against his better judgment.

"They sent me my call up papers for national service, and I didn't want to do it, so I just ran away to Liverpool where I knew there were other people from Trinidad, and I could disappear! We all came up here, the four of us in the band! You won't send me back, will you?" Rocke wasn't going to investigate him for the avoidance of National Service.

"I'm not interested in that, just solving this murder."

Warwick interjected. "But I can speak with my friends in London if you want Guv unless our friend co-operates?" For the first time, Warwick's intervention is useful and supported by Rocke.

"I will do whatever I can to help find this murderer, anything you need," offered Gus.

"That's good Gus. What time did you get back here?" said Rocke.

"I went for a walk after the Jac closed," said Gus, "and ended up in the Cabaret Artistes' Club until the sun came up. When I walked back here, I saw the police, so I panicked and came here, but Sammy didn't turn up!" He would soon find out why.

"No, he got lucky last night!" Warwick said with a smile on his face. Gus laughed for a moment, but the laughter soon faded away.

"What time did you get back here?" asked Warwick.

"I don't know, 9.30 maybe? I didn't do it; I promise!" Gus looked genuinely concerned that they thought it could be him.

"Just need to ask you some questions, that's all," reassured Rocke.

Gus felt the need to continue his own defence, even though he hasn't been accused or arrested.

"Please, believe me, I didn't do it; I wouldn't hurt Helen. I was at the club, and I can prove it. Just ask anyone there, I was there all night. I got drunk and fell asleep, and they threw me out this morning." Gus was dejected and sitting down again, leaning forward, looking at the floor.

Rocke then surprised Warwick.

"OK, Gus," he said, "we can check there. Can I trust you to stay here? Don't try to run away?" Warwick objected strongly to this course of action.

"But Guv?" he pleaded with his boss. "It's OK Warwick; he's not going anywhere, are you?" Gus reassured him.

"No sir, I promise." He had a look of hope upon his face that he was being believed. Rocke and Warwick got up to go, but Gus wanted a final word.

"Get whoever did this to Helen won't you?" he asked. After a short pause, Rocke turned to Gus.

"We will. Don't go anywhere, Gus." Rocke and Warwick left him and exited the building. Rocke called the constable standing outside the murder scene.

"Constable? Can you come here please?" He duly walked over to him.

"Yes sir?" he said politely. "There's a Trinidad musician called Gus upstairs in flat 2." He gave his clear instructions. "If he so much as tries to leave, slap him in cuffs and get him to the station?" The policeman wanted to make a good impression on his superior officer.

"Yes sir, my pleasure," he said proudly. He was overdoing it!

"Not pleasure, constable," he said sternly, "your duty." The chided constable is embarrassed and stood outside the house, ever vigilant to impress his boss!

Warwick caught on to what his boss was doing. "OK Guv, see what you're doing." Rocke is pleased that he was up to speed.

"Not just a pretty face Warwick!" he said with a smile. "Not enough evidence to place him at the scene, and I don't think, from his reaction, that he knew anything about it. He's probably not our guy!" Warwick wasn't totally convinced by his governor's decision.

"You're too trusting," he said. "Believe that stuff about dodging National Service?" The senior detective wasn't about to dismiss any line of enquiry.

"I thought you had friends in London?" he suggested to Warwick. "I assumed you would be asking questions anyway?" Warwick's face lit up.

"Well, I was just thinking..."

"Then do it Warwick - and we will know! I need to know how to get on to an American air force base, so let's get back to the station."

They returned to the car and headed back to the station.

Chapter Eight

The American Problem

As the two detectives walked back into Police HQ, the Chief Constable spotted Rocke and called him into his office. Warwick headed to an empty desk, as he still hadn't been allocated his own space yet, and got on the phone. Bell wanted an update from Rocke.

"So, what have we got so far?" he asked, settling back into his chair. Rocke remained standing as he answered.

"The victim had a man friend in the Caribbean band at the Jacaranda," he said, but before he could continue, Bell interrupted him.

"A black friend?" he asked a note of trepidation in his voice.

"Yes sir," was the reply, making the Chief Constable give a sharp intake of breath, and issue a warning. "Tread carefully, Rocke," he advised, which was quickly met by reassurance.

"I will sir, you know that," he explained, slightly aggrieved that he had to say it. "I've just spoken to him; he certainly has a motive, and we

need to check his alibi, but I don't think he did it."
Bell sighed with relief.

"There's an art student," Rocke continued, "who seems to have an intimate knowledge of the victim, but my main target and this is a tricky one, is a US serviceman from Burtonwood, who was the last person seen with the victim when he got into a taxi with her outside the Jacaranda Club and, according to the witnesses, against her will." Bell looked even more worried than he had at the beginning of the conversation. "We also found US currency by the girl's body," Rocke added.

Bell was taking it all in.

"US currency?" he asked rhetorically. "Interesting," he said, before pausing and thinking for a moment. "You want to go to Burtonwood, don't you?" he said, knowing full well what the answer would be. "Oh my God, Rocke, how are we going to get in there?" He took a long hard drag on his cigarette, and immediately grabbed his packet to light up a new cigarette.

"That was going to be my question for you," Rocke quipped. Bell was unsure.

"That's a diplomatic nightmare if we go in heavy-handed and start accusing an American citizen on American soil of murder!" Bell scratched his head, not sure which way to go.

"That's why I thought a telephone conversation between you, and the head honcho at Burtonwood might be the best way, no accusations, just a chat to help with enquiries." Bell saw the buck being passed.

"Thanks for that!" he said sarcastically. "OK, leave it with me. This should be fun." He reached for his telephone as he prepared to make a tricky called.

Rocke returned to the open office and headed towards his office as Warwick put his phone down and signalled he needed to talk with his boss.

"Guv, just spoken to my friend at the Met about our runaway," he said, his accent slightly stronger than before having spoken to his friend, "and he confirms that his name is on file, though they are not too keen on chasing him as they have other priorities!"

"Us too" his boss replied. "Well, he was telling the truth about that, so hopefully he is trustworthy and our instinct is right. The Chief is contacting Burtonwood so we will be able to go up there and chat to our American friend." The two men walked into Rocke's office and sat down.

"How long will that take?" asked the constable. "Don't know Warwick, but I don't expect it to be quick. Perhaps we should pop down to the hospital and check our friend Sammy's alibi to rule him out, and see what else we can find out about our victim."

Warwick was starting to enjoy working this case and continued the conversation. "And what about our art school friend who obviously knew her well? Maybe he was jealous?" Rocke was suitably impressed that they were starting to exchange some constructive dialogue.

"We can pop back down to the Jac this afternoon if your best friend Mabel is right," he said with a glint in his eye.

"Best friend?" he responded, with a hint of surprise.

"Got someone there who loves you Warwick!" he said smiling, but before Warwick had finished smiling, his boss hit him with the punch line:

"Had to find one eventually!" He couldn't help chuckling to himself at his own joke.

"But she's old enough to be my mother!" Warwick protested.

"Ah, maybe she sees a little lost boy in there?" Rocke smirked as he walked out of his office, followed by Warwick. They returned to the car and drove to the Southern Hospital at the bottom of Hill Street, where they parked up.

Before they left the car, Rocke felt the need to give some further guidance.
"Now remember, Warwick, this girl probably doesn't know about Helen yet, so tread carefully - don't put your big gob in it!"

As he climbed out of the car, Warwick asked his boss a question, which a look of puzzlement on his face.

"Guv? What is a gob?" Rocke laughed.

"It's the gaping hole in your face that you keep sticking your foot in!" he chortled. He locked the car as they crossed the road and walked up the steps of the Southern Hospital. They entered the hospital and headed for the reception, where he asked the young blonde receptionist for assistance.

"Hi, I wonder if you can help me? I'm Detective Inspector Rocke from the Special Section. I would like to have a quick chat with Nurse Dot Collinson, please. Is she free?" Warwick straightened his tie and made sure his hair was perfectly smooth, while Rocke removed his hat. The receptionist acknowledged the request and looked down her sheet filled with staff names.

"Er, yes sir," she chirped, "she is in Ward 8, which is on the second floor." She stood up to give directions. "Just follow the steps up there, and you will soon find it in front of you." She smiled as she finished giving her instructions.

"Thank you," he responded politely. Warwick smiled at the pretty receptionist but was soon beckoned by his boss to follow him. "Come on Casanova!" he called, almost dragging his sidekick away from the receptionist. Warwick smiled at her, and she blushed.

They found Ward 8 and looked through the small window into the ward. It was a long general ward with about a dozen beds on either wall, with a nurse's station in the middle of the ward, where two nurses were checking paperwork. As they had their faces up against the windows, they suddenly felt the wrath of the matron behind them!

"And what do you think you are doing?" she boomed. The two men jump out of their skin and became like naughty schoolboys in front of the head teacher! As one, they reply to her.

"Sorry matron," and look at the floor. She was a typical matron, in her late 40s, a stout woman who was only just over five feet tall, with a chest that would scare many a man.

"Explanation now, young man" she bellowed, "before I call the police!" She had obviously made that threat before.

"Erm, sorry, but we are the police." They both showed their ID cards to her, which she scrutinised carefully. "I am Inspector Rocke and this is DC Warwick." There was a brief pause.

"Am I supposed to be impressed by that?" she retorted. Rocke knew he had to get on her good side, but also discuss something delicate.

"Could we have a quiet word in private about one of your nurses?" he asked, but she was not for moving yet.

"Which nurse?" she demanded to know. He simply repeated the request with more authority.

"A quiet room, please Matron?"

She burst into her ward and marched the two policemen like naughty children to her office at the far end of the ward, through the far doors. All the patients stared at them, as they were only too fully aware. It had that unmistakable hospital smell of medication and disinfectant that conjured up reminiscences for the two men. The two nurses glanced at them as they passed by the table. They entered the matron's room, and Rocke waited for the matron to sit down, while Warwick stood by the door. The matron demanded an explanation!

"You come in here and ask to talk to me without an appointment, so this better be good!" she scowled as she shut the door.

"You have a nurse here called Helen Smith?" Rocke asked. She was quick to the reply.

"Yes, and she hasn't turned in again!" There was a brief pause before the questioning continued.

"Is that a regular occurrence?" he asked. The matron's mood was starting to soften as she noticed the sombre tone of the policeman's voice.

"Has been recently; at least three times in the last four weeks. What has she been up to this time?" she said, expecting to hear of a minor incident. She wasn't prepared for the reality.

"I'm afraid she was found dead this morning. She has been murdered."

There was a brief silence, and the matron's demeanour changed completely on hearing this news.

The fierce manner which greeted them initially had disappeared. Now there was only concern.

"What happened to her?" she asked softly.

"That's what we are trying to find out," he responded. "She was found in the entry behind a house in Selborne Street." The matron was now wishing to help.

"What can I do?" she enquired.

They needed to move on to talk to Helen's friend.

"I believe Nurse Collinson is a friend of hers who works here?" The matron looked out of the office.

"Yes, she is out there - they share a flat. Can this wait until the end of her shift?" she asked, but knew what the answer would be.

"Sorry matron," he said gently, "we need to speak to her now. Time is of the essence." Some of the fighting spirit returned to the matron.

"I'm already one nurse down!" she exclaimed, "This is very inconvenient, you know," Warwick chipped in sarcastically.

"Especially for Helen Smith!" he quipped. The point was made, and matron felt a little embarrassed.

"Let me bring her in, and we can tell her together?" she suggested.

"Whatever you think is best," Rocke replied.

The matron left the office and brought in nurse Collinson, a young girl in her early twenties, with brown hair and striking blue eyes. She was worried but wasn't sure why she had been summoned. Matron led her in and sat her in her chair. She started to shake with panic. Rocke looked at the young nurse

in front of him and obviously didn't relish the task he
had to perform.

"Nurse Collinson," he said kindly, "sorry to
bring you in here, but we wanted a bit of privacy.
You're a friend of Helen Smith, is that right?" She
looked startled.

"Yes, why, what's happened?" with a look of
panic on her face. Her bottom lip started to tremble.

"Were you with her last night?" he
continued.

"No," she replied nervously; I went home
without her." She obviously wanted to say more but
not in front of the matron. He was quick on the
uptake.

"Er matron," he said, looking at her directly,
"could we have a chat with her in private?" Matron
wasn't impressed but felt she had no option and left
the office. As the door shut behind her, the nurse
turned to Rocke, obviously ready to reveal more.

"What's this about?" she asked.

"Can you tell us who you were with last
night?" he asked, giving the impression that he
already knew something. She blushed and was
clearly embarrassed.

"I was with a friend," she said quietly, and
paused before adding, "a man friend."

Rocke had to be careful he didn't reveal too
much but needed to find out more.

"We have spoken to a man who says he was
with you last night and just want to confirm that.
Could you tell us his name?" he said, before saying,
"you're not in any trouble, don't worry, and nobody
else needs to know," he added, indicating he was
talking about matron. He looked at the matron
through the window and smiled, and she gave a smile

back, but was unsure why. This reassured Dot who felt willing to share more information.

"His name is Sammy," she said quietly, "and he plays in the Caribbean steel band at the Jacaranda." She wanted to make sure he knew she was a good girl. "I don't do this all the time; you understand," she explained.

"That's not a problem," he reassured her, "don't worry; we aren't interested in what you do or who with, just to confirm he was with you all night?" She felt comfortable talking to him, for some reason.

"Yes," she confirmed, "all night. He left for the Jac as I got up for work. Why?" She was unsure as to why he needed to know this information. He had to tell her.

"I'm sorry to have to tell you," he said formally, "that this morning we found the body of Helen Smith in the entry behind a house in Selborne Street."

Dot burst into uncontrollable crying and tried to talk through her sobbing.

"I knew something was wrong when she didn't turn up for work. This time was different - it wasn't like her."

Warwick produced a handkerchief from his pocket and offered it to the nurse, which temporarily threw Rocke. Dot had to ask the next question.

"Who did it?" If only they knew they could ease the pain of this young lady.

"That's what we are trying to work out," Warwick said, "so we need your help. Are you OK to talk?" She controlled her sobs and wiped some of her tears away.

"Whatever you need to know," she offered. "Did you think Sammy did it?" she said, a hint of fear in her voice.

"We just needed to make sure he was where he said he was," Rocke reassured her, "which you have done, so that is fine."

Dot then had a revelation as the information began to sink in. "Hang on, was it by Gus's flat?" she enquired.

"Yes," confirmed Rocke, "it was near there. What can you tell me about their relationship?" Now feeling more confident she was happy to answer the questions.

"Gus was so intense and Helen felt smothered by him. He was controlling and wanted to know where she was every day, but she wanted to be free, not tied down. It was a fun casual relationship for her, and she enjoyed being with him, but he was head over heels in love with her and claimed she was his girlfriend, but that's not how she saw it."

"Did they ever argue?" he asked, keenly awaiting the reply.

"They had a huge row last week," she said, "and Gus followed her home and was banging on the door in the middle of the night, telling her he loved her," and then she realised what she was saying and felt she had to put the positives of the relationship, "but he was more upset than anything else. He is a sweetie really, just loves Helen." This does nothing to stop this line of questioning.

"What did Helen do when Gus showed up like that?" Rocke asked.

"She came crying to me. She was upset and felt a little guilty." Warwick wanted to ask a question and stepped in.

"Was he ever violent towards her?" he asked, keenly watching Dot's face for a reaction.

"Oh no," she said reassuring them, "just lots of shouting. However, they made up again, and I thought that was it, but in the Jac last night, she told him in front of everyone that their previous encounter was a mistake, and I think she regretted making up with him." Rocke looked at Warwick making sure he knew not to butt in again.

"I believe there was an American with you all last night at the club?" This was the line of enquiry he was looking to pursue for now.

"They are fun to be around, the funny accent and yes mam, no mam, but nothing serious." Now he had to get specific.

"There was one guy, who was showing her lots of attention. Chuck was it?" he asked nonchalantly, hoping for confirmation.

"Yes, Chuck Warshowski." Warwick took careful note of his name. "Bit of a big gob really, but OK." At the use of the word gob, Warwick smiled now that he understood what it meant. "He was very aggressive and I don't think Helen liked it." Now they were making real progress on both suspects.

"And they went home in a taxi together?" he asked.

"They went off together in the taxi, but she never came home'; Dot responded.

"Did they have a relationship of any sort?" Dot was keen to put that one straight.

"No, he wanted to, and he did spend the night last weekend, but it was a one off." She then worried that it made Helen look bad. "She wasn't that kind of girl you know," she said emphatically, "I don't want you to get the wrong impression. Again, he wanted more, and could be very persuasive." Warwick stepped in once more.

"Verbally, or did he threaten her at all?" He wanted to know.

"He grabbed her by the arm a couple of times to drag her closer to him," she observed, "and she didn't like that. He is a big man, and she was certainly intimidated by him. Last weekend, they had a big row, and he slapped her across the face. I don't know how she could talk to him again. I don't want to get anybody into trouble, but I want to help you find whoever did this. I never liked that American. He always had his hands all over her and had a very short temper. All possessive, if you know what I mean? He could get physical and man-handled her a lot. He was always bragging about being a boxer up at the airbase and his great fights. I don't trust him." In her mind, it was clear who had done this: Warshowski.

That was all the policemen needed for now.

"Thank you, Nurse Collinson, we are just interested in finding whoever did this to your friend." He had one final line of enquiry.   "Did Helen keep a diary that you know of?" He was keen to know as much as possible to help them, and this could give them invaluable help.

"No, she had a little notebook, but no diary." This was obviously what had been found with her body.

"We found the notebook," he admitted, and she has a number of entries written simply as PB. Would you know who that was?" This could really help them.

"PB?" she asked, and paused to think for a moment, mouthing the initials PB to herself repeatedly. "Can't think of anybody with those initials," she added. "You sure it was PB?" she asked, obviously wracking her brain but to no avail. "Sorry," she said, "can't think of anyone." She was still thinking as Rocke decided to bring the conversation to a close.

"That's OK, don't worry," he reassured her, "if you think of anything else, can you give me a call at this number?" Rocke gave her a business card with his details on. Dot started to cry again, and this time it looked unstoppable. They were almost done now anyway, but he remembered he had to ask a vital piece of information.

"Did she have a family?" he asked, with Warwick standing there ready to take down any details.

"Yes, her mum and dad only live in Wavertree near us - she doesn't, erm," she corrected herself, "didn't, have brothers or sisters."

Warwick needed more details. "Do you have her parents' address?" he asked politely.

"Yes, it's 23, Newcastle Road, just by Penny Lane." Rocke immediately recognised the address, but it meant nothing to Warwick. He just wrote everything down.

"I know it - we will go and see them. We need to have a look at your flat if that is OK with you? Do you have a spare key?" Dot looked embarrassed.

"I know we shouldn't, but there is one under the plant pot. It is untidy, as I didn't get time to clean it this morning." Warwick again asked for the details.

"What's your address, Miss?" Again, she tripped over her words.

"We live, er, lived, erm; I live at 46, Penny Lane - ground floor flat." They had put her through enough for now. "Thank you, Miss Collinson," Rocke said, "I don't think we need trouble you any further today. If you think of anything else, let me know?"

Rocke indicated to the matron that she could come back in, as he and Warwick got ready to leave. The matron returned to the room and put her arm around Dot.   "Thank you, Matron, for your time and the use of your office too. Can I leave her in your hands?" The fierce matron was now the sweetest motherly figure anyone could wish to have.

"Of course, thank you. Come on Nurse Collinson, let's get you sorted out." She put her arm around Dot's shoulders and took her somewhere quiet. Rocke and Warwick left the office and walked back through the ward, all eyes on them again. They felt even more conspicuous this time. They exited the hospital, with Warwick waving a flirting goodbye to the receptionist. Rocke just laughed at him and shook his head. It was only what he would have done twenty years ago. They got back into the car to talk about what they had just learned. Again, showing no signs of decency or respect, Warwick puts his foot in it once more.

"Well, Helen seems like a real goer, doesn't she," looking for agreement from his boss, as laughed to himself.

"We are dealing with the murder of a young nurse," he said sternly, "so I don't think jokes are the order of the day, do you?" Warwick tried to plead his innocence.

"Just trying to lift the situation," he said, "no sense of humour some people," Rocke said.

"Time and the place, Warwick." Warwick decided it was time for a dig back at his boss.

"Sounds to me like our musician friend was not telling the whole truth, as I suspected. I told you we should have arrested him there and then!" He felt quite happy with himself.

"Stop trying to be smart Warwick," he snapped. "He is going nowhere."

Warwick muttered under his breath, though knew his boss could still hear him.

"You hope!"

Rocke turned to his wise-talking assistant.

"OK Sherlock," he said sarcastically, "tell me what we should do next?" Warwick thought for a moment.

"Elementary, Watson," he retorted continuing the analogy. "Go to the flat?" he said, though more as a question than a suggestion.

"We can do that later," came the reply. "What is missing?" he asked, waiting for the response. Warwick suddenly realised what his boss meant.

"Murder weapon," he said excitedly as if he was going to impress the teacher.

"Exactly, what was she strangled with because it wasn't there? However, first of all, I think we need to go and speak to the family and break the bad news. Please, no stupid cockney charm or pathetic humour. We are about to tell some parents that their only child has been murdered. God only knows what that is like!"

Warwick's face turned serious.

"I know what it is like," he said gravely. Rocke was surprised and stopped in his tracks. Warwick explained. "I am the younger of two brothers," he said with a touch of sadness to his voice. "My older brother, Michael, was five years older than me. When I was sixteen, we had the knock at the door from the police to tell us that he had been murdered." Rocke was looking at his new colleague in a different light.

"That must have been horrendous for them," was all he could think to say, before adding, "and for you too." There was a brief silence before he continued his story.

"It was, and still is. My mum cried for weeks, and my dad drank more and became more moody and quiet. Life changed. I decided to join the police to stop people having to go through what I witnessed. So, sometimes," he admitted, "I get a bit carried away and over-enthusiastic, but that is why."

Rocke wanted to find out more. "What happened to your brother's killer?" he asked.

"Never caught, but we had a brief description of him from an eyewitness. Around 20 years of age, nig...erm, coloured man in dark clothes, 6 feet tall, shifty eyes." Some things started to make sense to his boss.

"Is that why you have a natural distrust for black people?" he asked.

"Not the whole reason," he replied, "but I'm yet to meet many good ones," he said dismissively.

"I can understand that," Rocke said, "but hopefully you won't let that get in the way?" Warwick was happy to reassure his boss.

"No, Guv." His boss was happy to cut him some slack.

"But I do understand - and I'm sorry."

After a brief pause, Warwick asked a question which surprised Rocke.

"Can I tell the parents?" He didn't quite know how to respond to that request. He paused for a moment before responding.

"OK Warwick, if you're happy to do it, then that is fine with me." Maybe this was a chance to redeem himself.

"Thanks, Guv, I won't let you down."

Rocke started the car, and they headed off in silence to meet Helen's parents.

Chapter Nine

I'm So Sorry

The car pulled up outside the house, and the two policemen got out. They were both wearing sombre faces, as they dreaded what they had to do next. The house was a three bedroom, two-storey Victorian terraced house in the lower middle-class suburb of Wavertree, in what the locals call the Penny Lane area. There was no front garden, just two small steps leading up to the dark-blue   front door. Rocke knocked on the door and stepped back waiting for an answer. After a few seconds, the door rattled slightly as it was opened by a middle-aged woman, her hair in rollers, a stylish dress covered by a short apron where she had been cleaning the house. She was taken aback as she answered the door and suddenly felt scruffy and self-conscious. She couldn't work out who they were, mistaking them for salesmen.

"Hello, can I help you, gentlemen, though I'm not buying anything." She held her hand up hoping to dissuade them from selling her something she didn't want. Rocke had to check they were at the right house first, before proceeding.

"Yes, hello, is it Mrs. Smith?" he said politely.

"Yes," she replied, still unsure as to who they were. He introduced himself.

"My name is Detective Inspector Rocke, and this is Detective Constable Warwick. May we come in?" Her face became more serious.

"What's this about?" she asked, a puzzled look on her face. She was unaware of what was about to happen to her.

"May we step in?" he asked, not wishing to carry on the conversation on the doorstep.

"Of course," she said, inviting them in.

She opened the door and showed them into her front room, which was always kept spotless for visitors only - not even for her own family. It had a tiled fire surround, with a mantelpiece showing family photos of her wedding, Helen as a child and in her nurse's uniform too. At the centre was a dark-brown wooden clock. There was a radiogram in the bay window, an armchair in one recess and a three-seater matching sofa against the wall to the right. There was sun-faded wallpaper in a floral design on the walls and a large mirror on the wall to the left. A sizeable rug, a bit threadbare, dominated the centre of the room and had a mahogany style coffee table in the centre of it. There was the smell of furniture polish from where she had been cleaning.

"Please sit down, gentlemen. Is everything OK?"

She still hadn't worked out why they were there, which was going to make this even more difficult. Rocke indicated to Warwick to tell this poor unsuspecting lady the news that no mother should have to hear.

"Why don't you sit down, Mrs. Smith?" Warwick said, and by the tone of his voice, a look of dread came over her face, and she began to look pale. Warwick motioned to Mrs. Smith to take a seat in the armchair, which she did reluctantly and started to realise something bad was about to happen. "We are here regarding your daughter, Helen," he continued.

Almost as if in slow motion, as Warwick told her the news, the awful truth hit her. She started to tremble, and her bottom lip quivered.

"I'm afraid that we found your daughter's body this morning. We believe she has been murdered. We are so sorry."

After a pause, Mrs. Smith screamed a cry that only a mother can as she absorbed the news. She couldn't understand what was going on. Warwick suddenly panicked and didn't know what to do, and looked over to Rocke. He quietly told Warwick to comfort her, while he went to get some water from the kitchen. Warwick leaned down by Mrs. Smith and took her hand to console her.

"I'm so sorry to have to bring this terrible news to you," he said gently. He stroked her hand and amazed his boss as he re-entered the room. She had to know more.

"What happened? Who did this?" She wanted answers which Warwick couldn't give her.

"It's too early to say much. She was found in the back alley in Selborne Street...." and mid-sentence; Mrs. Smith interrupted him.

"Selborne Street? Near to Gus' place?" she asked, causing Warwick and Rocke to look at each other. Warwick was permitted to continue with a nod from his boss.

"You know Gus?" he asked.

Mrs. Smith regained her composure and as was typical of the lady, suddenly worried about everyone else.

"Lovely boy," she said. "Does he know?" She was obviously concerned about him.

"Yes," he replied, "we've seen him this morning, and he is helping us try to catch the murderer." Warwick knows he can't say too much.

"Who would do this to my baby?" She started to cry again, sobbing into the handkerchief. Rocke offered her the glass of water. She took a sip and tried to regain her composure again. She wiped her eyes, as she didn't want to cry in front of them. Rocke spoke.

"Mrs. Smith, you can be assured that we will not rest until we have caught your daughter's killer." His confidence reassured her.

"Was she, you know, interfered with?" She looked at him, hoping for the right answer. This was her tactful way to find out if she had been raped.

"We are pretty sure she wasn't, so rest easy on that matter." She breathed a sigh of relief. He continued his questions.

"Is there anybody in her life who has maybe threatened her, or she has mentioned to you that she is scared of?"

She thought for a moment, wishing to help if she could.

"No, nobody like that. She and Gus got on well, and all she talked about was Dot and work, though there was one mouthy art student who used to get on her nerves. Played in a band - she didn't like him, but I don't think it was anything. There was also an American who pestered her, which she didn't like, though I don't know his name."

Rocke and Warwick exchanged looks. Mrs. Smith needed to get on and be practical.

"I need to tell Mr. Smith. He's at work, and won't be home until tonight," she said stoically.

"Did Helen keep a diary? It might help us?" he asked. Mrs. Smith was quite definitive in her answer.

"No," she said adamantly, "she never liked them. She would always keep little notes in a book, but no diary." She then paused for a moment. "I can't say for sure since she left home, but I don't think she did. You could always ask Dot?" She was trying to be as positive as possible.

"We will do," he assured her. He then had to ask more questions and sensed that Mrs. Smith could cope. "Do the initials PB mean anything to you?" he enquired. She thought for a moment, mouthing the letters silently to herself, wracking her brain, but to no avail.

"PB?" she asked. "I don't think so, why?" Rocke felt it was OK to explain it to her.

"Helen wrote PB in her notebook a few times, and we wondered who or what it was." Again, attempting to be helpful, she tried as hard as she could, knowing that any clue could help find her daughter's killer.

"Nothing springs to mind; I'm sorry," she said helplessly.

"Not to worry," he reassured her, "thank you for your time, Mrs. Smith."

She stood up, with her typically British stiff upper lip, practical persona taking over. This is how

Liverpool women got through the war - we survived the blitz, we can survive everything.

"Thank you both for being so kind," she said politely.

"I will leave you my phone number which you can use to call me anytime," Rocke said, as he looked at the photograph of Helen in her uniform. "She was a beautiful young lady, and you should be proud of her."

That was the comment to tip her over the edge. Mrs. Smith started to cry again, and so they decided now was the time to leave her to grieve alone. She showed them out of the house. As the door closed, the two policemen heard Mrs. Smith burst into tears.

There was nothing they could do about it but resolve even harder to find the killer.

"Well done Warwick, you acquitted yourself well. Very professional - I knew there was a good copper in there," he said, not quite believing himself, but felt it was the right thing to say. He looked over at Warwick, who was still shaking and there was even a small tear in his eye. Rocke wouldn't mention it. They climbed into the car and didn't speak as they pulled away. As they turned to head back through the Penny Lane roundabout, Rocke broke the silence.

"As we are near, let's go into the flat and see what we can find," he said. Warwick was glad that the uneasy silence was broken, and hoped that his boss hadn't seen the tear in his eye. They drove down Penny Lane, looking for number 46. Warwick spotted it.

"Here you go, Guv, number 46."

They pulled up outside the house, which was a two-bedroomed Victorian terraced property. They exited the car and immediately looked for the plant pot that Nurse Collinson mentioned.   It was right by the door, and neither of the policemen were impressed.

"Seriously?" Warwick said, "Do you not have burglars up here?" Rocke was equally scathing in his remarks.

"Yes we do - can't believe how negligent some people are."

Warwick picked up the pot and retrieved the key. He opened the door, and they entered the hallway and turned into the front room, which was a typical student flat - not that clean, dirty cups on the table and plates on the floor, which hadn't been cleaned in days. There was a smell of food that had gone off, probably lying buried somewhere in the room. There was no fresh air either, which made it very stale. They held their breath for a moment, and Warwick even covered his nose and mouth.

"Do you think they are trying to find a cure for something in this lot?" Rocke asked cynically.

"I'm afraid to touch anything!" Warwick added. "Not much in here," he said, "I think we need to find the bedroom and discover if there really is a diary or any other clues!"

They walked through to the back room and into the bedroom. There were two single beds, with a bedside cabinet next to each one. Against the far wall was a traditional dark wood chest of drawers with a triple mirror on it. There were hairbrushes and makeup accessories thrown randomly on it, and assorted womens clothes on the floor, which they had to work around. Obviously, as Dot still lived there, they didn't want to pry too much.

Rocke sat on the bed and looked in the first bedside cabinet.

"Looks like this is Helen's," he commented. "There isn't much in this drawer, and definitely no diary." Warwick was looking on with interest, thinking that he wanted to look too as opposed to just standing around.

"Anything else in there?" he asked. Warwick sat on the opposite bed, looking around. Rocke suddenly sat up as he made a discovery.

"Here are some letters," he said, holding up a bundle of envelopes, "and they are addressed to Helen."

His interest was piqued as he opened an envelope and looked at the first letter. He examined it carefully, before reading the contents to his colleague.

"My dearest Helen, I can't thank you enough for sharing your time, and your body..." and he stuttered over the words, then Warwick interrupted his boss.

"Your body?" he said, his eyes lighting up. "Who is that from?" he asked, almost leaping over to the bed to sit alongside his Warwick, before Rocke held up his hands to back him away.

"Back off constable!" he shouted. "Erm," he added, Warwick sitting down again, "Arnold, whoever he is! 'I can't wait to see you next week!' it says, and it is signed with a few kisses too." They looked at each other.

"So, we have an Arnold," Warwick said. "Any more names there?" he asked. Plenty from him, and along the same lines. It seems like he is writing more in hope than expectation, but they obviously see each other regularly." They were slightly disappointed, hoping the search would be a bit easier.

"If only his initials were PB!" Warwick said, getting a nod of agreement in return.

Rocke found another letter of more significance.

"This one is from Gus!" he said excitedly. "Usual stuff," he added as he perused the contents of the letter, "but he is declaring his undying love for her, as expected. He continued to read on.

"Anything of any interest or relevant to give us a motive?" Warwick asked hopefully.

"He says that he has spoken with his parents, and he wants to take her to Trinidad. Now it is getting interesting."

"He thinks they're getting married!" Warwick said with shock on his face. Rocke realised the significance of what he was reading.

"And yet everybody else doesn't think they have much of a relationship," he said sarcastically.

"Seems to attract a lot of admirers doesn't she?" Warwick said, "but doesn't return the admiration to any of them!" Rocke retorted.

"Which must be frustrating," Warwick said slowly, thinking aloud, in tune with his boss.

"One of them must have snapped," he said excitedly, "she could have done that to the Yank too. Maybe Arnold and Gus could cope, but he couldn't!"

Rocke thought to himself for a moment and concurred with his colleague. "That would make sense." There was a moment's pause before Warwick spoke.

"Can't get passed those quarters found at the murder scene," he said, obviously still thinking of the American from the club.

"And we know she left the Jacaranda with him," Rocke said, their conversation flowing as if they'd been working together for years, yet neither of them realised it at the time. They just kept going.

"We need to check Gus' alibi and see if he really was at the other club as he claimed, in which case we can focus on our American friend," Warwick said. He couldn't decide if he suspected Gus or the American more.

Rocke decided they had to move on and keep the momentum going.

"And find out who PB is," he stated, indicating to his colleague to write it down, "plus this Arnold too." With his pen still poised, Warwick wanted to know if there was anything else to record.

"I take it, there was no return address on Arnold's letters?" he asked, more in hope than expectation.

"Nothing!" came the response. "Beautifully written, so he is a learned man. Good grammar and punctuation, even using semi-colons in their correct context!" The senior officer was impressed, but his junior was confused.

"Semi what?" he asked in a really strong London accent, sounding even more stupid as he asked the question, bringing a shake of the head from the junior detective.

"Semi-colons!" he stated in disbelief, "Did you go to school?" Warwick's reply brought a smile to Rocke's face.

"Sometimes, yes," his voice trailing off as he realised what he was admitting.

"Sometimes? God help us!" he said in despair.

"Somebody needs to!" Warwick added to himself, the mumble making its way to his boss, who just grinned.

Realising they were not going to get anything else from the flat, Rocke made a decision. They needed to make some headway, and he knew where to start.

"Right, let's go and find our musician friend and bring him in for a chat. If it was Gus, and I only say if, he wouldn't have had much time to get rid of any evidence, so we will need to get a good look around Sammy's flat and out the back of the house too."

With a nod of agreement, they left the flat, replacing the key under the plant pot and getting back into the car. They drove off, heading towards Selborne Street.

Chapter Ten

He's Done A Bunk!

As the car pulled into Selborne Street again, the constable was still outside the house where Gus was staying. Rocke exited the car closely followed by Warwick. He went to talk to the constable. "Anything happened since we were here?" he asked.

"Nothing sir," he replied promptly, "nobody has come or gone since you left." Rocke was happy but just thought to check with him again. "Is Higgins still around the back too?" he said starting to walk away but was stopped in his tracks by the response.

"No, he left about 20 minutes ago, sir," he added. Panic struck the faces of Rocke and Warwick as they looked at each other, Realising that Gus could have escaped at the back.

"What?" he yelled, starting to run. "I told him to stay there!" he shouted angrily. "Right, Warwick you go around the back, and I will go in here and hope he hasn't done a bunk." Warwick needed another translation.

"Done a what?" he asked, looking confused.

"Not now Warwick! Go!"

Warwick ran around the houses to the alley at the back, while Rocke entered the house through the front door again, let in by the same lady who had been looking out of the window at them behind her curtain. He ran up the stairs to Sammy's flat, and the door was open. He went in slowly, checking to see if his target was anywhere to be found, but and there was no sign of Gus. He checked every room, slamming the doors into each one, but there was no trace of him. He went over to the back window where he could see his colleague in the alley. Warwick opened the gate into the back yard, a small concrete paved area at the back of the house. He spotted his boss at the window and shook his head, letting him know that Gus could not be found there either. Rocke kicked the nearby chair in anger and frustration.

"Damn it!" he yelled as the chair flew across the room.

Rocke opened the window to shout to Warwick.

"Have a look around in case there is any evidence of any sort there," he yelled, making sure he could be heard. "I will check here, but I think he has legged it."

He then had a thought and changed his mind.

"No, change that," he said, "you stay here and have a good look around. I think I had better go and break the good news to the Chief!"

As Rocke moved away from the window, Warwick had a little smirk to himself. Without looking out, Rocke shouted to his constable,

"Wipe that smirk off your face, Warwick!" Warwick was non-plussed. How did he know? He gave up trying to work out how he did that, then began a search of the backyard, looking in the rubbish bins, coal house and outside toilet, without any success. He continued to search as Rocke returned to his car and headed back to HQ to face the wrath of his Chief Constable.

Chapter Eleven

Dog Tags

"So you're telling me you lost him?" Bell screamed as he paced up and down his office, with Rocke sitting in a chair, simply taking the flak. "Our number-one   suspect, and you left him alone? What were you thinking about man? You're a smart guy, and I back you, but this is ridiculous!" Rocke waited for a pause before it was safe to speak.

"I didn't think it was him," he explained, "but I left a police guard front and back so he shouldn't have been able to get out! Some fool told the constable to leave the scene after I told him to stay there."

He stood up, put his hands on Bell's desk, and looked straight at the Chief.

"If I find out which idiot did it, then there will be hell to pay."

Bell stood opposite to him, put his hands on the desk and bellowed his response.

"Well, that idiot was me, Rocke!" His face was getting redder,   and the colour drained from his opponent. "You told me he wasn't your suspect," he continued, pointing a finger at Rocke, pushing the blame onto him, "so I told Higgins to come back. We don't have a huge budget, as you know, so I gave the order."

He relented, and sat down again in his chair, suggesting that his colleague did the same. Rocke was obviously embarrassed by his outburst and would like to take it back! He had to apologise.

"Sorry sir, it's just that I didn't think it was him." He had placated his boss, and because of their friendship, they could both forget it happened.

"But why do you think it is him now?" asked Bell. "What changed your mind?" he continued. Rocke thought for a moment, before putting his case.

"I still don't think it is him, but this makes him look suspicious," he explained. "We went to see the victim's friend and flatmate who said that there was a big argument last week, and then they sort of made up. I just need the whole story from him, so we need to find him as soon as possible."

Bell seemed to understand, and wanted to progress the case, so he moved the conversation onto the subject of the 'Yank' that Gus thinks did it.

"On the subject of the American," he said, "I have managed to get you an appointment tomorrow morning at Burtonwood, but" he said seriously, "listen to me mate, there are very strict boundaries for this meeting."

He counted off the conditions on his fingers as he went through the list.

"No wild accusations, no allegations, no interrogation or unsubstantiated threats. It is investigatory only. Play this wrong and there could be huge repercussions, so tread carefully."

Rocke nodded in agreement to every stipulation as if it was not a problem. In his mind, he was thinking the opposite but wouldn't say so.

"You report to Major Ratcliffe, who will need some convincing to let you take this any further." Bell passed Rocke the info he needed on a piece of paper. He took it, checked it over and placed it in his pocket as he stood up.

"Thank you, sir, will do. Just got to keep Warwick quiet!" He gave Bell a knowing look as he said it.

"How is he doing?" Bell enquired. He wasn't quite ready for the response.

"A young, gobby racist who speaks his mind too often and is one threat away from a punch from me," he said with more than a hint of sarcasm in his voice.

"Good," said Bell, as if oblivious to what had just been said, "I thought you two would get on!" He couldn't help smirking to himself.

"You do this on purpose don't you?" Rocke said mockingly.

"Me?" said Bell innocently, "no idea what you mean!" He was chortling to himself by now. He couldn't help but have one last dig. "Try not to lose any more suspects please!"

As Rocke started to leave the office, he responded to that quip.

"And try not to take my constables away from their duties!"

"Touché George!" said Bell, laughing to himself.

They both smiled as Rocke left the office and headed back to his own office. When he closed his door, he kicked his small metal rubbish bin across the room in frustration, and paper fell out all over the floor. He looked out of the window to the Philharmonic Dining Room, his favourite local pub, and felt in need of a pint. He lit a cigarette and took a long drag, while he thought through everything. However, that pint would have to wait, as he had a killer to catch, and with his number-one   suspect on the run. Just then, the phone rang on his desk. It was the police surgeon.

"Rocke," he said as he picked the phone up. "Hi John - excellent, come on up."

He picked up the rubbish from the floor and put it back in the bin, which now has a big dent in the side where he kicked   it. He checked that he hadn't thrown anything important out and got a bit lost in thought for a moment. As he placed the bin back down, McKenzie knocked at the door and came in. He immediately spotted the dent in the bin and chuckled to himself.

"Haven't lost the power in your right boot then?" he said, laughing at his colleague. Rocke smiled - his short fuse was well known among his friends. He took another long drag on his cigarette and felt he should explain.

"Bad morning!" he grumbled. McKenzie decided to rub salt into the wound.

"Lost a suspect have you?" he chuckled. He couldn't miss the opportunity.

"You know," he sighed with more than a hint of exasperation, "this station has a better intelligence network than my snouts! Maybe I should ask one of them who did it," he shouted while pointing to his colleagues in the office. "They know everything else!"   All the heads in the office had turned around at his outburst and were staring at him. He glared back and shouted at them.

"Get on with your work!" with which the usual hubbub and general noise returned to normal.

They both laughed and sat down.

"Give me some good news, John?" he pleaded.

"Well," he pondered for a moment. "My initial thoughts were right. She was struck at the back of the head, giving her a subdural haematoma, which would have stopped her in her tracks." There was a brief pause, when Rocke realised the implication of the statement, having spent so much time with McKenzie.

"But that didn't kill her?" he asked, looking for approval from the doc.

"Well spotted George," he said, giving him the nod of approval. "No, it was asphyxiation as I suspected. A tight ligature, maybe a piece of thick string or something like that, quite thin, as the bruising is restricted to something about a half inch wide at most. It was crudely done, and probably wasn't that quick, so the poor girl suffered."

Of course, what George wanted to know, and what Helen's mother needed to know, was: was she raped?

"You mentioned at the scene that there was some redness at the top of the thigh. Was there a sexual assault?" John was quick to reassure him.

"She had intercourse last night," he said, "but there was no sign of assault, so I would say it was consensual." George breathed a sigh of relief. "There were traces of semen," McKenzie added, "but not of a prophylactic, so it was probably impulsive too." Rocke thought over the implications.

"Sounds like our American friend was lucky then," he said, with a hint of sarcasm in his voice.

"American?" McKenzie asked, and then remembered his discovery in the alley. "Those quarters?" he asked. "Where does an American come into it?" Rocke was happy to enlighten him.

"She was seen leaving the Jacaranda in a taxi with a US serviceman."

With that, McKenzie started to laugh.

"Burtonwood?" he said chuckling away to himself. "Ha! Good luck with that one!" Rocke was not as amused.

"I know. Bell has got me in there tomorrow!" McKenzie continued to laugh at his friend's expense.

"Try not to start another war, please!"

"Basically, John," he stated in his best Queen's English accent, "I've got to go in there, not question him, not accuse him, and ask him if it isn't too much trouble, would he mind awfully confessing to murder!" McKenzie gave a hearty laugh at Rocke's mock posh accent and explanation!

"Well, that would work, George," he said, with a little chuckle still in his voice.

Rocke needed to get back to the matter at hand.

"Okay, John, the joke is on me!" The grin disappeared from McKenzie's face. "So, what about the time of death?" The doctor checked his notes.

"I would estimate that it was between 1.00am and 2.00am. How does that help, if at all?" Rocke shrugged and sighed.

"Well, doesn't really help much." He stood up, took another drag on his cigarette, and ran his fingers through his hair. His friend wanted to help more.

"Wish I could tell you who it was, pal," he said, closing his file of papers, "but that's your job! I wouldn't want to make it too easy for you!" he said, laughing.

"I'm sure I used to think of you as a friend!" he responded, allowing himself a little laugh at his own expense.

"Well George, I will get this typed up," he said, waving the report in his hand, "but I don't think there is too much more I can tell you to help. I assume there is no sign of any more evidence from the scene?" he asked.

"I've left Warwick there," he said, raising his eyebrows at McKenzie.

His friend wanted to find out what that expression meant, as he stood up.

"How is he doing? Any improvement?" he enquired. Rocke sighed to himself.

"Don't get me started on him! You may be investigating his murder by the end of the day if he doesn't pull his socks up!" McKenzie laughed as he left the office, and Rocke couldn't help chuckling too! He stared out of the window again, trying to think about what had happened so far. The silence was interrupted by a knock upon his door. Standing there was a red-faced Warwick, who was out of breath and panting hard.

He was gasping for air while trying to talk in short breaths.

"Guv, you've got to see this," he eventually said, before taking a huge gulp of air into his lungs.

"What's up with you?" his boss said, staring at this wreck of a policeman, many years his junior, in front of him.

"When was your last physical?" Warwick ignored the sarcasm and told his story.

"I've run down with this because I had to show you what I found near the flat." He pulled a small bag from his pocket and placed it on the desk. Inside are the dog tags that were worn by US servicemen. Rocke lifted it up and examined it carefully. He took a magnifying glass from his desk to try to decipher the inscription. As he brought it into focus, he read out the name.

"Warshowski. Charles Wm. USAF."

Naturally, Rocke needed to know more.

"Where was this?" he asked quickly, desperate for the information. Warwick was proud of his find and wanted to make it sound as good as possible to impress his boss.

"It was by the drain, partially hidden," he said, re-enacting every move with his hands to demonstrate how clever he had been, "but by the back gate, just into the alley - erm entry," he corrected himself, much to Rocke's amusement, "and it was just lying there." He paused for dramatic effect, before his big finale, "The sun just glinted on it and it caught my eye. No blood or anything on it." This was a Major find, and Rocke became excited and was reinvigorated.

"So our American friend was in the entry near the murder scene; we must assume with our victim. So why was he there, with her, nowhere near her flat, and certainly nowhere near his base?" He clapped his hands together with joy. "A breakthrough, Warwick, well done." The junior detective was happy with the praise and carried on the conversation.

"And why was it outside the flat where Gus was holed up!" he stated, making his boss think again.

"But" he said, "Gus said he was in the Cabaret Artistes Club all night." Warwick was on a role now.

"How could he be, Guv? The club must have closed in the early hours, even with a lock-in."

How naïve the young lad from London was.

"The Cabaret Artistes Club is not a normal club," Rocke pointed out. This left Warwick a little confused, and not for the first time that day.

"What does that mean?" he said, "a club is a club, even if we turn a blind eye, they still close by 2 or 3 in the morning." Things were different in Liverpool, as he was about to find out.

"It is what we call a 'shebeen', Warwick," he said. "Ever heard of them?" The look on his face said enough, but he still answered.

"Never, Guv." His boss was about to enlighten him.

"It is our term for an illegal strip club! We 'turn a blind eye' as you mentioned, because they keep the riff-raff off the streets. And, this one, in particular, is only around the corner from Selborne Street on Upper Parliament Street." Warwick realised the significance of it.

"So Gus could have sneaked out," he said, as if a light had suddenly gone on, "murdered Helen, and gone back to the club." He thought for a moment. "Do they have a doorman?" he asked.

This was not an easy question to answer.

"Every club does, but they don't keep a record," he said. "We need to know if he really was there all night or not." Another lead and one that could be very important.

"What's the plan Guv," Warwick asked?

"We need to go to the club, but they don't seriously open for business until after 8pm. Tell you what," he suggested, "let me introduce you to some fine ale and great pub food, and you can buy the first pint!" Warwick's eyes lit up. After all, he thought, some of the best work was done over a pint.

"Do you have proper beer up here?" he asked cheekily.

"Higsons is one of our best local brewers," he said proudly. "As you're buying, you can be the judge!" he retorted with a grin.

They left the office and crossed over the road to the Philharmonic Dining Rooms, which had ornate gold gates at the entrance, with the interior decked out like a luxury liner from a bygone age. With oak-panelled walls, opulent light fittings and chandeliers, it was one of the finest hostelries in Liverpool and conveniently situated across the road from Police Headquarters.

Chapter Twelve

I'm Not A Racist

They walked into the pub and straight to the bar. Many of Rocke's colleagues were already in there on a 'long lunch' and said hello to him, whilst eyeing up Warwick, who stood out like a sore thumb. The barman caught Rocke's eye immediately.

"Usual George?" he shouted from behind the bar.

"Yes please Ted," he responded as if greeting an old friend, "and the same for the lad, here" he added.

"Got another one?" he said with a smile.

"Yes, don't know what I've done to deserve it, but this one is a southern Jessie!" The jokes were at Warwick's expense, and he could do nothing about it.

"Not a Cockney" Ted asked with a hint of sarcasm to his voice, feigning shock?

"Fraid so" George sighed.

"Actually," Warwick interjected, "I'm from North London and not a cockney." He had obviously taken offence to being called a Cockney, but the others continued the joke.

"All the same to me, you all look and sound alike!" Rocke said sharply.

"What do you mean by that?" he responded angrily, his facing turning pale and serious, and had clenched his fists. The irony of the comment suddenly dawned on Warwick, and maybe his colour prejudice had just come back to bite him on the bum!

"Sorry me old mucker" Rocke said in a mock London accent, "Maybe we should send him back to where he came from?" He clearly aimed the remark at Warwick while talking to the barman.

"Sounds good to me," Ted replied.

Warwick laughed and realised this was an initiation, and that he had been hoisted by his own petard. The pints appeared at the bar, and Rocke picked his up and motioned to Warwick that it was his round. With one look, Warwick took his wallet out and paid for the drinks. They took their glasses and went to sit in a nearby snug to talk.

"Cheers Warwick," he said, raising his glass.

"Cheers Guv," he responded, "and point taken." He had to concede he had been caught out.

"So what did happen in London to get you sent to the 'outback' of Liverpool?" he asked.

Warwick set about telling his story.

"This nig....." and then he stopped mid-word and corrected himself, feeling the glare from his boss, "this coloured guy was always on the take and my snout told me what he was planning and where, so I got there to stop him, but he ran for the embassy. He was just short of the American Embassy steps when I caught him and got him to the floor. He threw something into the embassy which must have been the knife that he had used to kill a young girl. I had to get him because he had been on the run for weeks, so," he took a quick drink from his pint, and then a guilty look came over his face, "I got some evidence from the crime scene and planted it on him. I had to get him; he was guilty Guv; he was a murderer." There was a brief silence with Rocke aghast before he exploded.

"But you didn't have the evidence," he shouted, slamming his pint on the table, and causing so much of a stir that conversations finished and everyone stared at their table. It was eerie silence for a moment before Rocke looked around and everyone's head turned away, and they restarted their conversations. Warwick had to justify himself now.

"I know," he protested, "but we had to get that guy off the streets." His boss was not convinced.

"Agreed," he said, "but you have to build your case and get the evidence together." He had bent a few rules over the years to get his man, but planting evidence was not acceptable.

"I know it was stupid," he admitted, looking genuinely shamefaced, but Rocke wasn't finished.

"And racist!" he exclaimed.

Warwick wasn't prepared to accept that.

"I know I have used dodgy language and terms that have annoyed you," he admitted.

"And are unprofessional," Rocke added.

"But I'm not a racist," Warwick protested, "I just think that mixing cultures causes confusion and unsettles people." The conversation continued to be more philosophical than it had started.

"Each to their own culture," Rocke pointed out.

"Exactly," Warwick said, pointing a finger at his boss. "Keeps it simple. That's how it works in

London and works well." He was quite happy with his point of view.

"Well, this isn't London," the Liverpudlian detective said, which brought a muffled response from his southern colleague.

"Ain't that the truth!" That brought the conversation to a natural conclusion.

"Right, where are we with the murder?" Rocke said. "Let's think about this. We've got a dead nurse, who sometimes dated a black musician and others..."

"Plus liked our American friends," Warwick interrupted.

"Including Mr. Warshowski," Rocke continued, "whose dog tags were found at the scene - hang on," he said, as if something suddenly dawned on him, "you didn't plant them there did you?" He couldn't help smirking as he said this and Warwick at first was about to get annoyed, then, Realising it was a joke at his expense, smiled too.

"OK, fair cop Guv." They both laughed and took a sip of beer.

"Sorry, couldn't resist!" The two were warming to each other and maybe that rebellious element in Warwick's character reminded him of himself when he was a young detective.

"If we look at our American friend, we've got his dog tags; we know he left the Jacaranda with the victim, there were the US quarters by the body. Everything points to America!"

Now it was time for Warwick to get his own back. "And we've lost our prime suspect whose story is looking less credible as the day has progressed!" He'd succeeded.

"Well, maybe I got that wrong, so I will hold my hands up to that one," he said honestly. "But" he emphasised, "he can't get far, and I'm still not convinced he is our guy." This got Warwick slightly agitated.

"Why?" he shouted, the pitch of his voice getting higher. "Means, motive, opportunity, dodgy alibi, skipped from the police," he said confidently, before landing the last blow: "what else do you need?" Rocke let his assistant calm down, left a dramatic pause, and then answered the accusation.

"Convincing, Warwick! The first thing we have to do is visit the Cabaret Artistes Club and check his alibi, and then we will know better, won't we? Anyway, the evidence says it is our American friend!" He slapped the table and stood up. "Drink up!" he commanded.

"I've only just started this one!" he complained.

Rocke laughed.

"Slowcoach - can't even handle your drink!" He started walking away, waited for his colleague, and talked as they left the pub. "Where are you staying by the way?" Warwick caught up with his boss before answering.

"The Adelphi," he replied. Rocke was aghast.

"How did you get in there? That's the best hotel in town!" Warwick laughed as he realised he had got away with a cosy number at the hotel.

"I think the Chief was desperate to get me up here quickly," he said as if he was in demand. He was fooling himself alone of course. "It's only for a couple of days. Got to find my own digs after that." His boss was a bit happier with that news.

"Well, we can look at that tomorrow. Come on, let's go to a strip club!" He stopped in his tracks and thought over what he had just said. "Can't believe I said that."

He shook his head as they walked back to his car.

Chapter Thirteen

The Stripper

They drove along Upper Parliament Street, looking for the club. Warwick was taking everything in, obviously not knowing where he was. It was dark and dry and there were a few people walking down the road.

"So where is it we're going" asked Warwick?

"We are going to the Cabaret Artistes Club," said Rocke, "which is where Gus said he was last night. Now this is a strip club, and it is run by Allan Williams, who owns the Jacaranda, and his business partner Harold Phillips, who owns the Colony Club, and who is better known locally as "Lord Woodbine."

"Sounds like a man with a smoking problem," said Warwick sarcastically.

"That's what many people wrongly assume, Warwick. He is one of the most respected men in the community. He was born in Trinidad and even joined the RAF at the age of 14, before returning home. He then returned here from Trinidad on the *Empire Windrush* in 1948, with a couple of calypsonians, known as Lord Beginner and Lord Kitchener. That is why he was called Lord Woodbine, not because of cigarettes, but because he was a calypso star. He can sing and play, especially the steel pans."

"Sounds daft to me," said Warwick dismissively.

"Everything sounds daft to you, Warwick; you have no interest in anything that isn't about you and your prejudices!" Rocke was clearly disgruntled.

They passed a couple of buses as they drove up the hill.

"On the right is Berkely Street where Lord Woodbine's Colony Club is. The Cabaret Artistes Club is further along here. Rocke slowed down, looking for the building.

"Right, the club is along here on the right-hand side at number 174a, according to their advert." Warwick couldn't resist a joke at his boss' expense.

"Like you've never been here before?" he said sarcastically. Quick as a flash, Rocke responded.

"Steady Warwick or I might leave you in the middle of nowhere to find your own way back!" He chuckled to himself at the prospect while wiping the smile of his apprentice's face.

They pulled up at the side of the road and got out of the car. There was a faint sound of music coming from the basement of 174, Upper Parliament Street. They walked to the iron railings outside the house and there was a small gate, with steps leading down to a door. They walked carefully down the steps and knocked on the door. A big black man, obviously the doorman, peered through a small opening at head height.

"What you want, man?" he said in a deep, West Indian accent.

"I want to speak with the manager," Rocke said.

"Are you colour prejudiced?" the unembodied voice said, ignoring the question.

"No, I'm not," Rocke said defiantly.

"Well I am!" the voice replied, and then the small opening suddenly slammed shut.

Rocke, unimpressed, got his warrant card ready and knocked again on the door. Warwick thought this was hysterical, and couldn't help chuckling to himself! Once again, the slat opened and the doorman was presented with a warrant card.

"I will ask you again - can you open the door and take me to your manager, please?"

The doorman closed the slat, but then they heard a couple of bolts being slammed and a chain removed before the door opened slowly with a creak. Rocke and Warwick walked into a very dark room filled with men who are watching a well-endowed, buxom lady stripping to a small band of four musicians - two guitars, bass and drums. The musicians, not well known, were referred to as John, George, Stuart and Paul respectively - standing around a little stage, which was dominated by the stripper. The music wasn't impressive, and the audience of men were not interested in the group, just the lady removing her clothes.

The two men walked across the back of the room, and the doorman introduced them to a smartly dressed Trinidadian gentleman. The doorman spoke quietly so as not to panic the patrons.

"These two gentlemen are from the police,"
he said discreetly.

The doorman then turned to Rocke and
Warwick.

"This is Matthew, who manages the club," he
said.

"Er, shall we go into my office, gentlemen?"
Matthew said in a strong Caribbean accent.

They walked across to a petite room in the
corner, loosely referred to as an office. It had a small
wooden table, a chair, a couple of photos on the wall
and a free-standing metal safe. There was a table
lamp which was providing a bit of light. Matthew sat
on his chair, and Rocke closed the door behind him.

"What can I do for you?" he asked.

"Is Lord Woodbine not around" asked Rocke
inquisitively?

"No, he's performing with his band at the
Colony Club tonight, where he is most nights,"
Matthew said, trying to be as helpful as possible.

"Well, my name is Detective Inspector Rocke,
and this is DC Warwick. We are investigating the
death of a young nurse called Helen Smith."

Rocke was surprised by the response.

"I heard about it - she was at the Jac last
night." Warwick and his boss exchanged looks.

"How do you know that," Rocke asked?

"From Allan Williams, who owns the Jac," he
said, which helped settle the policeman's nerves. "He
told me," Matthew continued. "John and the group
were there last night too and talked about a fight, but
that was all they knew," he added. With that
information, something rang a bell in Warwick's
mind.

"John," he said quickly. "Guv, didn't the cleaner tell us about a John, who knew her?" This meeting was taking an unexpected twist.

"I would like to talk to John, I think," he said to the manager. "When are they finished?" he asked.

"Well," Matthew let out a dirty laugh that was infectious. "Janice is very popular - she will only undress to live music, you know, not records. That is a touch of class!" The policemen weren't as impressed as the manager was.

"Class" Warwick said in shock? Rocke thought he should move the conversation on.

"We were talking to a friend of Helen's, Gus Woodrow," he said, allowing a slight pause to gauge a reaction, "who says he was here last night?"

There was no delay in the response.

"Gus," he asked? "Yeah, man, he was here. Got really bad and fell asleep here. We had to throw him out this morning!" he said as the intonation to his voice reached a high pitch.

"What time did he get here?" Rocke asked. Matthew thought for a moment and looked at the clock upon the wall as if that could tell him.

"About 12.30 this morning," he said.

"Can you confirm he was definitely here all night. Any witnesses" asked Warwick quickly? Matthew laughed again.

"Yeah, man," he said, waiting for the revelation, "me! I took the decision to leave him here all night, and then opened up this morning and chucked him out! He was here all night, for sure!" He was confident in his replies as if that was all that was needed.

"And what time did you leave?" Rocke asked him. Suddenly, the witness wasn't so confident.

"I have no idea," he said, shifting slightly uneasily in his chair, "but he was here when I left." Again, the questions were not finished yet.

"And you locked him in," he was asked?

"Well, erm, I suppose I might have done, but I can't be sure." Warwick was straight in.

"What do you mean, you 'can't be sure'?" he demanded.

"Well, it doesn't really lock from the outside, and I didn't want to lock him in, just in case he wanted to go home, but he was here at the same place when I arrived this morning." This wasn't good enough for the young policeman.

"So you can't be sure if he left and came back or not? He had a few hours to sneak out and come back again to provide an alibi."

Matthew leapt to his friend's defence. "No way, he wouldn't do it." Rocke looked the manager in the eyes with a fierce, fixed stare. Even Warwick was surprised by the steely look on his boss' face.

"But you can't prove it, can you?" Rocke said sternly. He let those words hang in the air. Matthew had no answer to that - he couldn't prove that Gus was there all night, and was starting to panic.

"Look," he said nervously, "you're not going to close me down are you?" His eyes went between the two policemen anxiously.

"We might," replied Warwick, "depends what happens, so don't bank on it!" Rocke glared at Warwick for speaking out of turn, signalling that he should be quiet.

"We are after a murderer, so this isn't a priority for me, but maybe think about your stay-behind policy?" Rocke's eyes told Matthew all he needed to know.

The music stopped outside and there was a loud cheer and clapping, plus the unmistakable sound of wolf whistles from the appreciative audience.

"Is that it finished" asked the inspector? Matthew nodded and made a quick suggestion.

"I would stand to one side if I were you, sir."

With that, the door opened and the stripper, clutching her clothes to cover her nakedness dived into the small room and disappeared behind a curtain in the corner of the room that they hadn't even noticed in the dark. Warwick and Rocke couldn't help looking at the stripper as she passed by. They are slightly shocked and Matthew just chuckled to himself!

"Welcome anytime gentlemen, as my guests," he offered, not expecting a positive response.

"I think I'd like to talk to John from the band please," was the only comment Rocke was going to make.

Matthew led them out of the office and up to the stage, which now had some light shining on it, though not enough to see the musicians clearly. The men among the audience could spot a policeman easily, and all covered their faces and headed toward the exit.

"That's the end of the night for me - thank you for nothing!" Matthew said, who was clearly frustrated. They walked up to the stage where the musicians were tuning up and trying to look professional. John was clearly the leader and Matthew introduced them to him.

"John, this is detective - what was the name again?"

"Rocke," he said formally. John couldn't help but look for a chance to have a joke at the policeman's name.

"And I suppose he is 'roll' is he?" he joked, pointing at Warwick while looking to his band-mates for a laugh. "We don't need any more Rocke 'n' roll," he said, the others laughing with him.

"From what I heard I'd say you do!" the inspector responded quickly. John liked to spar and realised he had a worthy opponent!

"Touché, Sherlock, what can I do for you?" He seemed happy to co-operate.

"We just want to ask you a few questions about your friend, Helen Smith," he said.

John was happy enough to talk as he sat back onto his amplifier that was leaning against the wall.

"Yeah, she was in the Jac last night," he said, "looking as gorgeous as ever." He looked at his friends who all laughed along.

"Do you see her there often" the detective asked?

"Unless we're working, getting gigs, busy people," he bragged as if he was a professional musician constantly in demand. Rocke looked around as if to show he was not convinced by John's blarney!

"I'm guessing you're there a lot then?" Rocke said. John laughed, as he knew he had been caught out.

"All the time at the moment!" he said with a sound of resignation in his voice. "Saw Helen last night too, with some American." That brought the conversation nicely onto where the policemen wanted it.

"We were told that you shouted something to Helen as she crossed the room. What was it,

Warwick?" Warwick checked his notebook carefully, finding the page with the exact quote, which he read precisely.

"Nice to see you with your clothes on," Warwick stated clearly. John laughed to himself and his friend Stuart, standing next to him, laughed along. "Good one John!" he said, still laughing. The others joined in with the joke too.

"What is so good about that" said Rocke judgmentally? "How long were you seeing each other, or was it just the occasional fling?"

John was slightly bemused by the question and so decided to have a bit of fun with the detective.

"Last time was yesterday morning," he said, almost re-enacting every movement, "and she stripped off, and I just stared at her naked body for about two hours." By this time, John was licking his lips, obviously pretending to lust after the image of Helen's body.

"More like two and a half hours, John," Stuart said. With that, Rocke and Warwick looked at each other and were more confused than ever.

"That half hour was me on my own, eh Stu?" He nudged his friend, as the banter continued.

"Half an hour," said Stu, "What did you do for the other 27 minutes?" Stu gestured with his hand whom he knew what John was doing! Lennon slapped Stuart playfully, and he fell over as they laughed. "Mind that wrist John," continued Stu, "you're going to need it!"

Rocke had to regain control of this conversation as he was losing it. "Hang on," he said, "who are you? You were there too?" This didn't make sense.

"Stuart Sutcliffe. Yeah, I was there too." John continued to confuse the police.

"Plus about ten other lads and what, seven girls I think, Stu?" The lads continued with the banter.

"Eight John, don't forget Cyn," Stu answered.

"My favourite Cyn of all, may God forgive me," said John, his play upon the word 'sin' continuing to add to the confusion. John looked angelic and placed his hands together as if praying and gazing to the heavens.

"You having a larf," said Warwick in his strongest London accent. John instantly found another victim and began to mimic the detective.

"You having a larf. Cor blimey, Leave it out, Guvnor." Warwick was offended and obviously angry. The other lads laughed at John's humorous skit. Rocke just motioned to Warwick to calm it and decided to put an end to the frivolity.

"OK, we've had a good laugh. Now, start talking. When was Helen Smith your girlfriend and how did it end?"

There was a brief pause before they all began to laugh at Rocke's suggestion.

"No," John laughed, "she wasn't my girlfriend! She was a life model at the art college! Hence, 'didn't recognise you with your clothes on.'"

John and Stuart laughed out loud at the misunderstanding. Paul and George joined in laughing at the policemen's expense. The penny dropped with Rocke. He had got it wrong, but he realised he needed to know more.

"Erm, er," he stumbled as he regained control of the conversation and continued his questioning. "How long has she been modelling there?" he asked.

John thought for a moment, looked at Stu, before answering.

"For a few months. Good extra pay for her in between shifts!" Now they were getting somewhere.

"How did she get that job?" he asked, Warwick, taking everything down.

"Old 'Doggy' Barker tapped her up at the Jac," he said as if the policemen would know who that was.

"Who is 'Doggy' Barker?" he asked John.

"Tutor at the art college," he responded helpfully.

Warwick wanted a dig at John and chipped in sarcastically.

"What's his real name," he snapped, "he can't have been christened 'Doggy' can he?" He picked on the wrong man!

"Maybe his mum was a bit 'ruff'," he said, bringing a laugh from his friends, "a bit 'barking' mad?" The other lads laughed again, and Rocke couldn't resist a smirk, which he tried to hide from his colleague.

"Look, John, it's good to have a laugh, but I'm afraid that I have some bad news." The laughs died down as they realised something was seriously wrong. "I'm afraid Helen is dead."

The atmosphere changed completely, and the smiles wiped off all of their faces. John, in particular, was shocked, almost in disbelief.

"Dead?"

John looked around and in a split second his compassionate side was showing and the start of a tear formed at the corner of his eye, but he couldn't let his guard down in front of his group. He was visibly shaken. He started to pace up and down in front of Rocke, repeatedly saying, "fuck, fuck, fuck......" Rocke wasn't sure how to react to this sudden change.

"I'm afraid it is true. Her body was found this morning." John started stumbling over his words as he wanted to find out more.

"Well who, what I mean, what the.........." John struggled to put his words together and tripped over each syllable. "How did it happen? Where did she die?" He was getting angry and kicked a chair over.

"Well, at the moment..." Rocke began to talk before Lennon turned really aggressive and lost his temper.

"Don't fuckin' mess with me, whatever your name is, tell me what happened. I guess that it wasn't natural causes if you're here." He was clearly agitated and becoming worse.

"Come on John, calm down a bit and let's talk."

John slowly stopped pacing and returned to his seat, but was still clearly unnerved. Rocke started to tell him a bit more to see how he reacted. Was the reaction because he knew what was happening or shock?

"Her body was found in the alley in Selborne Street this morning," he said.

"Selborne," he replied. "That's just round the corner isn't it?" Warwick made a quick note: 'knows where Selborne Street is'. His colleague answered the question.

"Yes. About a five-minute walk from here." John was more conciliatory and now wanted to help, but his anger was growing by the second, though he was keeping it more controlled.

"She didn't do anyone any harm," he said, "nice girl, a good laugh, but she wasn't herself last night at the Jac. Normally if I throw that line out, she comes back with something funny, but she didn't, she was just, I don't know, a bit weird! She's a great girl; I just can't believe..." For once, John was almost lost for words. "She didn't deserve this; she didn't do anyone any harm, why would they; I mean, Helen, I........." John stood up defiantly, before declaring, "if I find out who did this, I will kill them!" You could cut the atmosphere with a knife. Rocke broke the silence.

"Not the best thing to say to a policeman!" John suddenly realised what he had said.

"You know what I mean!" Stuart put his hand on John's shoulder to console him.

It seemed clear enough to Rocke that John was telling the truth. "Look, help us find who did this. Now, this art tutor, Barker, what's his full name?" John was suddenly tongue-tied and looked for help from his friend.

"Its, Arnold, isn't it Stu?" Even he wasn't so sure, having only ever referred to him by his nickname.

"Yeah, think so," he offered. Rocke and Warwick exchanged knowing looks. "Yeah, Professor Arnold Barker," said John, suddenly remembering.

"And he usually frequents the Jac does he," John was asked.

"Most of the tutors do," he confirmed, "we all hang out together."

"Just in the evenings?"

"No, afternoons too when we can - saves doing any work!" They all laughed.

"Alright for some! So, what did you lads do after the Jac closed?"

John felt an accusation may be building here and got defensive and stood up straight defiantly.

"Hang on, no way did any of us do this, not to Helen. You better not be suggesting anything."

"No, no, calm down son, that wasn't an accusation, just trying to build a timeline and find out who did what and when so we can eliminate as many people from this as quickly as possible." It did the trick, and John was happy to help.

"Me and Stu went back to our flat in Gambier Terrace, and Paul and George went early to get the last bus home, didn't you?" Paul and George nodded in agreement before Paul thought he should clarify it, perhaps unnecessarily. "Yes, I live in Allerton and young George is in Speke." George didn't like the fact that Paul had referred to him as 'young'.

Warwick was making notes. John then began to tell his version of what he saw.

"Now, Helen was sitting with this arrogant American, big fella, there with a couple of his mates, and Gus wasn't happy about it. Got to say Helen was a prick teaser........she took him half the way there if you know what I mean?" The other lads laughed with John, but Rocke kept the questions coming.

"And Gus didn't like it?" he asked. John wanted to support his friend.

"No, but he wouldn't harm Helen; he is mad over her, and he is a peace-loving man, especially the amount of stuff he smokes...." Warwick latched onto the drug reference and jumped in.

"So he's a drug user then is he, this Gus?"

His boss glared at him because this distraction was not helping.

"He smokes the occasional joint," John admitted, "but that just makes him even more peaceful! He wouldn't harm a fly! It couldn't be him," John protested, so he tried to deflect the attention onto the other suspect.

"But that American," he snarled, "Helen, Gus and the American went outside and there was a big argument going on! Helen didn't want anything to do with either of them, so Gus withdrew, but the American pushed Helen into the taxi and got in behind her. She wasn't happy at all; I know that. I should have stopped him!" John was getting frustrated and angry, and obviously prejudiced. "Don't trust them Americans - wouldn't catch me going to America!" The others agreed with him.

Rocke decided to move on. "Tell me more about Professor Barker?" Stuart decided to add his opinion to the conversation.

"He's been at the art college all his life, I reckon," he said, "must be in his 50s." As Warwick made notes, his boss continued the questioning while they were being so co-operative.

"And is he married," he asked. John took over answering again.

"No, the gay bachelor; loves the single life and loves his women. Dirty old man preys on the young nurses to..." John suddenly realised what he was saying. "Wait a minute, he likes the ladies," he said, wanting to clarify his comments, "but it's nothing to get hung about. He likes the attention, as they do too, an admiring older man buys a few drinks and asks the pretty ones like Helen to be life models for us to draw, paint and dream about!" John had piqued the policeman's interest now.

"And Barker approached Helen and asked her to be a life model?"

"Yes, she needed the money because the nurse's pay isn't great."

"Well, hopefully, he can help us a bit more and see if we can find out more about Helen from him. Anything else you can think of that might be relevant?"

"Don't think so, but I'd look at that American if I were you. He fancied invading some foreign territory if you know what I mean!" The lads laughed at his latest joke. John also wanted to preserve his reputation as a rock 'n' roller. "By the way, don't tell anyone we are doing this gig!"

"Why not?"

"We are a serious rock 'n' roll group, and only doing this to help Lord Woodbine out. He and Allan Williams are managing us now and have got big plans." He didn't sound too convinced himself. Warwick felt it was time for some of his humour.

"Serious rock 'n' roll group? From Liverpool? I'd get used to playing strip clubs if I were you!" This didn't help things at all, just making John angrier.

"Well you're not me, and we are going places and trust me, after this week, we are never playing a strip club again, ever!"

"I hope they're paying you well?" Rocke added, but Paul obviously wasn't impressed enough!

"You bet they are! We take the money for the indignity of it!"

"Yeah, must be hard," said Rocke.

"Or am I just pleased to see you," said John quickly? The others laughed. Rocke couldn't help liking John, but Warwick just didn't get the humour at all.

He just looked bemused by it all. "Just for the record," said Rocke, "what do you call yourselves?" John stood up proudly.

"The Silver Beatles," he said.

"John and the Silver Beatles, like Buddy Holly and the Crickets?" John wanted to clarify things.

"Yeah, but we are just The Silver Beatles." Warwick wasn't impressed.

"Never get anywhere with a name like that," he scowled.

"You just wait - we are going to the toppermost of the poppermost," and the others joined in with a shout of 'yes!' Warwick laughed at John's cockiness and sneered at him with derision.

"Good luck with that, you'll need it!" he muttered to himself. Rocke stepped in to diffuse the potential fight.

"Anyway, thanks lads for your help." They all muttered in acknowledgement, and then turned their backs and carried on tidying their gear away.

Rocke and Warwick turned and started to walk back towards Matthew when John, for once being serious, calls after Rocke. "You will find whoever did this won't you?" The response was swift and reassuring.

"You can count on it son. And Matthew," he said, "thank you for your hospitality and your help." A smile spread across the manager's face.

"My pleasure man, I hope you catch the guy. Don't pay no attention to John, he's all talk, but they are a good group!" The policeman laughed.

"I like them too - just don't tell them I said that!" The two men laughed as they shook hands and parted.

The policemen exited the club and returned to Upper Parliament Street where they stopped for a quick chat. Warwick obviously had something on his mind that he wanted to say.

"Why do you let people like that big mouth talk to you like that, Guv?"

"Because, Warwick, he's all gobby in front of his friends, but if you listen carefully, you'll hear what's really going on. You've got to know the culture of Liverpool. Up here, we tell it how it is, man to man, face to face. You can't bully them into submission because here we learn to fight with our mouths before we can punch!"

"No respect, if you ask me!"

"But think what we learnt by exchanging a bit of banter with him. I think we can safely rule him out, and while everything points to our American friend as Gus seems to have a good alibi, I want to talk to Professor Arnold "Doggy" Barker as well."

"Barker just sounds like a dirty old man to me."

"Barker likes the company of young nurses and gets them to take their clothes off for money." He let that thought linger for a moment. "That's enough for tonight - we've got a trip to America tomorrow, and that is not going to be easy. Come on, I will drop you off at the Adelphi and them; I'm heading home."

"By the way, did you have the same thought as me about Barker's initials?"
"Yes, Professor Barker - maybe he is our PB?"

"That's what I was thinking!"

"You thinking, Warwick?" he said sarcastically. "Well, that's a good start!"

They walked to the car, Rocke smiling at his own wit, and Warwick lost for words as usual.   They climbed in and drove off.

Chapter Fourteen

Home At Last

Rocke's car pulled up outside a 1930s semi-detached, four-bedroomed house in the Liverpool suburb of Allerton, and he got out, tired after a long day at work, but that was nothing new. He walked through the cast-iron gates, up the driveway, and looked over his front garden with pride. He mentally relaxed after a stressful day, and took a deep breath, then smiled as he was home. He arrived at the door, turned the key and walked into the hall, where there was a flight of stairs going up on the right-hand-side. He passed the front room door on the left and into the lounge in the back of the house. There was a dark mahogany fire surround in the centre of the far wall, and wall lamps in the alcoves either side of it. Above the fireplace was a large mirror, and in the far corner was a small television within a wooden surround. A three-piece suite dominated the centre of the room, and in the left-hand corner of the room, in the armchair, was Rocke's wife, Emily.

Next to her in the recess was a small table with a lamp on it and in front of the lamp was a wireless. She was listening to Radio Luxembourg while reading a magazine. Emily was the same age as Rocke, though looked younger, and was also a Liverpool girl. By day, she was a secretary at a solicitor's office in Liverpool City Centre and was immaculately dressed as ever. In spite of ten years of marriage, they, alas, had no children. She was so lost in reading her magazine and listening to the wireless that she didn't notice her husband come in. He could smell his dinner and took a big sniff to try to identify the beautiful odour.

He coughed in the doorway, and she jumped with fright!

"George," she yelled, playfully, "you scared the life out of me!" She stood up and smacked him with the magazine in mock anger.

"Sorry to disturb you, Queenie!" They both laughed and he gave her a peck on the cheek.

"So where have you been," she enquired?

"Hanging out with some musicians at a strip club," he said casually, knowing what his comment would do. He let the phrase sink in. She picked up on it straight away.

"You've been where? Another boy's night out?"

"Not a chance! Grubby little place on Parli," the local name for Upper Parliament Street, "investigating a murder, I'm afraid."

"And you just had to go to a strip club," she said, looking dubiously in his direction.

"It's hell my dear, but somebody has to do it!"

Emily walked into the kitchen and disappeared for a minute or so before returning with a hot meal for her husband and herself. They sat at the small mahogany dining table against the far wall, set for two people, poured a glass of white wine, and began to eat.

"Is this a bad one, George?" she asked.

"Yes, sadly. Young nurse found strangled in the entry behind Selborne Street."

She was shocked and saddened.

"Oh God, no. Poor thing." They sat for a moment in silence, and took a sip of wine, before beginning to eat.

"I know, Queenie. Not straightforward, and one of our suspects, who I thought was under house guard, skipped out the back!"

No matter how he worded it, she knew what he meant.

"You lost him?"

"Yes," he admitted with embarrassment. "The Chief pulled the constable standing outside the back of the house, so the suspect just walked out!

"Do you know where he is?"

"No!"

"And you think he is the one?"

He paused for a moment, before answering.

"You know," he said pensively, "this morning I thought no, this afternoon I thought yes; his alibi is reasonably solid, but I can't rule him out."

"And you've got to do this on your own, haven't you."

"Oh no, forgot to tell you," he said excitedly, "I've been given another DC to help me!"

There was a pause.

"And," she said, needing more information?

"He's a young, bigoted, racist Londoner, who is on his final warning! Just what I need!"

"Oh no, why you?" She had genuine sympathy for her husband.

"That's what I said to the Chief!" he exclaimed, putting his cutlery down and holding his hands out like he was a real victim. However, he did concede that Warwick had his good points. "There's a decent copper in there somewhere - he just keeps it well hidden!"

They both laughed as they continued with their meal before Emily returned to the case.

"So, what are you going to do next?"

"Going to Burtonwood tomorrow!"

"To the base," she said with surprise?

"Yes, need to talk to one of their servicemen who likes to come into town and cause trouble."

"And I suppose you've got 10,000 possible suspects?" she said laughing. "Those servicemen are nothing but trouble."

"I know," he said, "and the Chief has had to swing some big favours to get me in there, so I have to be very careful what I say - don't want to start world war 3!"

"I wouldn't worry; they will still turn up late as usual!"

They both laughed as they finished and their meal, and relaxed for the evening. Emily always knew how to be a sounding board for her husband, and help him relax after a stressful day.

Chapter Fifteen

America, Just Outside Liverpool

It was a fresh morning in Liverpool as Rocke pulled up at the front of the Adelphi Hotel, where Warwick was standing, waiting for the car to pick him up. He walked over and opened the door.

"Morning sir," he said to his boss, who was surprised at being called 'sir', as opposed to 'Guv' which he had had to put up with all day yesterday. He didn't expect that to last. They headed off for their meeting, for which Rocke was very nervous. The drive took about 45 minutes, and the two policemen talked generally about the case so far, catching up on what had happened the day before.

As the car pulled up to the entrance of the US airbase at Burtonwood, he had to lay a few rules down.

"OK Warwick, best behaviour or else we don't get to talk to our guy, and the shutters go up!"

"That's OK Guv; you can rely on me. I don't think he's our guy anyway." If that was supposed to help, it didn't.

"Everyone is a suspect until we rule them out," he exclaimed.

"Including Gus," Warwick retorted. There was a pause: how did that go down?

"Fair point Warwick." He got away with it.

As they pulled up to the gate, they could see a gatehouse with two white US servicemen holding machine guns. However, there was some commotion behind them with dogs and dog handlers appearing from the trees along the boundary to the right. In front of them was the airbase. Huge hangars and workshops could be seen, as could the rows of dormitories where the servicemen were based. The car stopped at the gate, and a guard approached Rocke.

"Can I help you, sir?" the guard said with a southern drawl to his American accent.

"Yes," he responded, "Detective Inspector Rocke to see Major Ratcliffe." The guard went to check his roster to see if the policeman was on that day's list of visitors. He soon returned to the car.

"That's fine sir. If you follow the road round to the left," he said, showing the driver the way, "you will see the HQ with the stars and stripes outside it."

"Thank you," he responded, before trying to find out what was going on with the dogs.

"Have you got problems?"

"Nothing for you to worry about, sir."

The gate was lifted and Rocke drove through, following the directions. They both kept looking at the commotion to see if they could find out what was going on. In the meantime, the guard rang through to HQ to let them know to expect their visitors.

"This place is like a town in itself," said Warwick, almost in disbelief at what he was seeing.

"It's a home away from home, a little part of England that will be forever America," said Rocke sarcastically.

They pulled up outside the main building where the stars and stripes flew proudly from a white flag pole in the wind. An officer walked out to greet them.

"Good morning," he said, "I'm Major Ratcliffe." He had a totally different accent to the soldier on the gate, but Rocke couldn't place where in the US it could be from.

"You must be Detective Inspector Rocke." They shook hands warmly.

"Yes, thanks for agreeing to see us. This is Detective Constable Warwick." They nodded to each other.

"Please come in," he said in a friendly manner.

So far, so good. They walked into Ratcliffe's office and sat down. Everything was organised neatly, and Ratcliffe sat in his chair behind a large oak desk. Ratcliffe was in his mid-50s with neat, black hair and a stylish moustache, that reminded the two policemen of the latest Hollywood stars. There were photos of his family on the desk and a phone. He gestured to his guests to take a seat. They sat down in a wooden chair facing the Major.

"So gentlemen, have you heard of Burtonwood?" he asked.

"I have, but Warwick here has only just moved to Liverpool, so a history lesson wouldn't go amiss for his sake."

"Well Warwick," Ratcliffe said, standing up and straightening his jacket, "RAF Burtonwood was established here in April 1940 as an Aircraft Storage Unit and in 1942 was handed over the US Eighth Army Air Force as an ASU making Burtonwood the largest military establishment in Europe. At its peak in 1944, 18,500 American servicemen were based at Burtonwood. A total of over 15,000 aircraft were processed at Burtonwood during WWII, and the site was re-manufacturing over 2,000 aircraft engines each month. After the war, thousands of surplus US aircraft were scrapped here before the US Air Force left in 1946. However, Burtonwood was handed over to the Americans as a support for the aircraft of the USAF based in the UK and Europe. Two years ago, flying ceased here, but we have continued to use the base as a supply and storage facility unit."

"So, how many personnel do you have here," Warwick asked?

"About 7,000 at present."

Rocke was still curious about the commotion at the gate.

"There seems to be something going on as we arrived - have we come at a bad time?" He thought by being polite he could really find out what was going on.

Ratcliffe was keen to dismiss it.

"Oh, it's nothing really. We think an intruder got in last night as there was a breach in the fence at the far side, but that's not unusual. Normally local guys being dared to get inside the perimeter without being caught." He hoped that would be the end of it.

Rocke just put it on the back burner for now. "So, what can I do for you gentlemen?" the Major asked.

"A young nurse was found murdered yesterday morning in Liverpool," said Rocke, "and the last person to see her alive was one of three US servicemen with her in the Jacaranda Club in Liverpool City Centre."

"Now hold on Inspector," the Major said, immediately going on the defensive, "I hope you're not accusing one of my men of committing homicide?"

"Absolutely not, Major," he reassured him, "we are just at the beginning of our enquiry, and he is not our prime suspect at all, but he should be able to help us with the timeline and help us catch the real killer. His name is Warshowski, and I wondered if, in your presence, we could just chat with him?" His diplomacy saved the situation, and the Major calmed down again.

"Not a name I know personally, but that isn't a surprise due to the large number of personnel we have here. Hold on a moment, I'm sure we can arrange something, but you do understand that you are effectively on US soil, and therefore, I will just remind you of your lack of authority here." The two detectives nodded as the Major spoke. "I am more than happy to offer you every courtesy to assist you with your investigation, but I reserve the right to stop you if I think you have overstepped the mark."

Rocke held his hands up to show he was more than happy to comply.

"Of course, Major."

Ratcliffe went to the door and spoke to his assistant.

"Can you get Warshowski here?" he called out. Rocke just gave Warwick a knowing look. A voice came from outside of the door. "Yes, sir." Ratcliffe returned to the room.

"Do you have much trouble with the servicemen on leave," Rocke asked? "I'm not aware of any particular issues; you understand, as I tend to only be involved in serious crime, so haven't had the need to come here before."

"We did have trouble a couple of years ago when the men went into town together. It often ended in fights between them, but not much more than that. These guys are thousands of miles from home, and where there are women, there will be fights, but no more than high spirits." The men smiled knowingly.

"What did you do to stop it, Major," Warwick interjected?

"On this site, detective, we operate segregation, so the coloureds and whites are kept apart. When we sent them into town together, they would fight each other. So, we tell the coloured men to find their own clubs for coloureds, which are in a particular area I believe." The two policemen are lost for words.

"You have a segregated base," Rocke asked in amazement?

"Yes sir," he replied proudly, "and it works." Warwick seemed happier about the way they did things here.

There was a timely knock on the door, and a young US officer entered out of breath. Ratcliffe is shocked and a little embarrassed.

"Captain O'Rourke, what's the matter?"

"Sir, it's Warshowski. We've just found his body," the Captain said.

Everybody stood up at once in shock to look at the Captain.

"What do you mean, body, Captain? Explain yourself."

"They've found his body," he explained, "which was hidden among the trees. He didn't get back to camp until 2.30am, but when he didn't turn up for roll call this morning, we began searching for him." This was highly embarrassing for him in front of the British policemen.

"Why wasn't I informed of this, this morning, Captain?"

"We didn't want to cause alarm - assumed it was a simple matter of oversleeping."

Rocke wanted to offer his help.

"Major, this can't be a coincidence. How can we help?"

"Sorry, Superintendent," he said acerbically, "but we have our own ways of dealing with this."

"But this is clearly linked with the murder of the girl," he protested. "He was the last person seen alive with her, and now he is dead."

The Major thought carefully, before making his decision. "OK Superintendent, come with us, but as observers only." He was quite adamant, but the detective was happy just to be invited to be there.

"Absolutely, Major," he reassured him.

They exited the office and clambered into the Captain's Jeep, which sped off to the murder scene.

Chapter Sixteen

A Dead Suspect

As the vehicle pulled up to the scene, there were dogs barking, and two servicemen standing by the body. They immediately saluted their superior officer's arrival. Warshowski was lying in the dirt, face up. Major Ratcliffe walked up to the officer standing by the body, who also saluted.

"What the hell happened here," he asked?

"Looks like he has been strangled sir, quite crudely, and severely beaten. There has obviously been a struggle."

Rocke had moved towards the body and appeared alongside the body.

"Major, if I may examine the body?" he asked, more in hope than expectation.

"That's not protocol, Superintendent," he responded but was obviously considering the request.

"I have seen the other body, Major," he said, "and I can see if there are any similarities. I won't interfere with the crime scene."

"OK Superintendent, we may need to help each other."

Rocke knelt down by the body, and the first thing he checked for was the dog-tags, which of course he knew was missing.

"No dog tags, Major."

"That's most irregular," he replied.

"Actually, we already have them." This comment drew surprise from the Major.

"What?"

"It was one of the points for discussion today, which we hoped he would be able to answer. We found his dog tags at the murder scene of the young lady."

"And now he is dead too," observed the Major.

"Exactly!" Rocke spent a short time examining the body in front of him, before giving his initial assessment. "He appears to have been beaten and involved in quite a struggle. However, this is different than the murder of the girl. That strangulation was neater, more organised. This is rushed, more amateurish, not the same at all, though of course we are comparing the murder of a member of the armed forces and a nurse, so we can't rule out the possibility of it being the same man." Rocke then made a discovery. Beneath the left shoulder of the dead man, partly buried beneath the soil, was a gold ring. He picked it up with a pen he had taken from his pocket and held it up to show to the Major.

"This is a grand ring, quite bold and even opulent. Not many people I know would wear a ring

like this, eh Warwick? Seen a similar one recently?"
Warwick thought for a moment, and then suddenly
realised he had seen one like it before.

"Gus," he suddenly recalled. "He had a
couple of really big rings, didn't he?"

"He certainly did Warwick, and one was
missing from his right hand. I noticed the skin was
used to having a ring on it, there were marks beneath
the knuckle."

"You know whose ring this is,
Superintendent," asked Ratcliffe?

"I am sure we do. May I take this with me?"
he asked. "I am confident we will have the murderer
in custody very soon!"

"That is not the way we do things here, but if
you give me your word that you will apprehend the
culprit, then I am prepared to give you leverage, but
keep me informed Superintendent."

Rocke stood up and shook the Major's hand.

"You have my word, Major. Can you confirm
the time Warshowski got back to base was 2.30am?
That would be a help too."

"Sure thing."

"Thank you, Major, you have a lot to do here.
Shall we keep in touch, as we can probably be of help
to each other in clearing these murders up? Can you
let me know what your post-mortem reveals?"

"Sure. Let's talk later. Captain, see these
gentlemen back to their car."

"Yes, sir."

The Captain led Rocke and Warwick back to
the Jeep and drove them back to Rocke's car in
silence; Rocke and Warwick exchanged looks. This
had suddenly become even more complicated. They

climbed into their car and headed towards the exit, with the camp in chaos.

"Well, that's made it a bit more interesting, hasn't it Warwick?"

"A dead Yank! And one of our prime suspect's dead!"

"Didn't expect that. What happened in that entry last night for him to lose his dog tags?"

"Keeps coming back to Gus for me."

"I know; we need to find him, but he has an alibi. Surely he can't have been missing for that long from the club, to kill Helen, then come all the way out to Burtonwood, kill Warshowski and make it back. Doesn't make sense to me. There must be somebody else."

"PB?"

"Exactly! We need to speak to the Professor as a priority. Maybe he is framing Gus? However, where does the ring come into it?"

"The ring was very easily found."

"Thank you, Warwick!"

"No offence, Guv, but you didn't have to look hard, did you?"

"Good point - you mean it was meant to be found?"

"To put Gus in the frame and keep us away from the Professor. It makes sense."

The car drove off into the distance as the two policemen contemplated what they had seen and churned it over in their minds in complete silence for most of the journey back into Liverpool.

Chapter Seventeen

Guess Who Just Confessed?

Rocke sat behind his desk, smoking a cigarette while listening intently to the voice on the other end of the telephone. He suddenly became animated and grabbed his pen and scribbled as he talked.

"Thanks, we can be there at 4.30pm, and tell him not to worry, we just need a bit of help with our enquiries." He waited impatiently, but politely, to complete the niceties to terminate the call. "Thank you again for your help." As he put the phone down, Warwick ran into the office very excitedly.

"Guv, you've got to get down to the interview room now," he said, panting.

"And what's got you so excited, Warwick?"

"You'll never guess who just walked into the front desk?"

"Go on, astound me?"

He pulled himself together and began to speak slowly and deliberately.

"Gus Woodrow."

Rocke was genuinely astounded, and for a moment was lost for words.

"What," he said incredulously? "Just walked in?" He stood up, still in shock. "Why?"

"He says he wants to confess."

"Will this day get any more confusing? Oh well, what are we waiting for, then?"

Rocke straightened his tie, extinguished his cigarette and put his jacket on before they headed down to the interview room, where Gus was sitting in a sparse room, with just a chair facing the door with Gus on it. There was an empty chair next to him, two empty chairs opposite him, and a PC by the door standing guard. Rocke and Warwick walked in and sat down at the table. Warwick had a writing pad with him, and Rocke had a file with photographs and paperwork in it. He slapped the file on the table noisily, making Gus jump, then sat down, all the while staring at the man in custody before him. He pulled the chair in, made himself comfortable, and took a deep breath before beginning the interview.

"So, Gus, have you been advised of your rights," Rocke asked?

"Yeah man, I don't need no solicitors. I come to confess."

"Well, Gus, I have to warn you that anything you say may be taken down and given in evidence against you."

"I know. Just write it down and I will sign it."

"Talk me through last night. Why kill the woman you supposedly loved?"

Gus was taken by surprise at the statement from Rocke.

"Whoa, what do you mean, woman I loved? I didn't kill Helen!"

Rocke and Warwick are as confused as Gus! They looked at each other and then back at him.

"Well, what have you come to confess to?"

"I killed the Yank! He killed Helen, so I killed him. That's what I come to tell you."

"You admit to killing Warshowski?"

"I sneaked out of the house this morning and into the alley, and I found his dog tags. He did for Helen, so I got him."

"And how did you do that?"

"I went up to Burtonwood and passed a message to a friend of my auntie who is on the base. I told Warshowski that I knew what he'd done and had his dog-tags and to meet me by the fence. However, I realised I didn't have his dog tags. I must have dropped them."

"We found them in the alley," interjected Warwick, much to his boss' annoyance. "Where did you find them?"

"They were almost falling into the drain," he answered. "I saw the light shine on them, so I picked them out and saw his name. I knew it was him."

"Did you see him do it," asked Rocke?

"No, but I saw them leave together; she didn't want to go, so he took her there, raped her and then killed her."

"How do you know that?"

"I just know," he said emphatically.

"Helen wasn't raped," Rocke said slowly and deliberately, to gauge the reaction.

Gus was momentarily confused and was clearly thinking about a response.

"But he killed her," he repeated, trying to justify his own actions.

"Why would he take her there, Gus? It's nowhere near her flat or where he lived?"

The interviewee was clearly becoming more agitated.

"I don't know," he cried, scratching his head. "I just know he did it. Why else would his dog tags be there?" He was becoming desperate.

"We have no proof that he was there, Gus, apart from the dog tags that ended up there, and you could have planted them there."

"After killing her," Warwick said, pointing a finger at him. "Maybe you were just covering your tracks and trying to blame somebody else."

"Then why would I come in here and confess?" he pleaded. "I could have escaped and never come back, so why would I come here? I avenged Helen so now we are quits. So lock me up, I don't care no more. I'm saying nothing else now."

Somehow, call it a hunch, but Rocke wasn't convinced by what he was hearing.

"How did you do it?"

"Not saying nothing!" He folded his arms defiantly.

"Answer him," shouted Warwick.

"No," he retorted, "just charge me, and I sign it. Saying nothing more!"

"OK Gus," said Rocke as he stood up, and closed his file. "You will be charged with the murder of Warshowski."

He then walked out, but Warwick was almost more confused than when they went in. He followed

Rocke out wanting to know why the interview was cut short. They walked down the corridor and headed back to Rocke's office.

"What's going on Guv, why cut it short? He confessed."

"He did."

"And surely he killed Helen, because who else would take her there, kill her there and then plant the evidence? He shuts Warshowski up, probably intending to put the blame on him, but his conscience got the better of him. Why don't we just charge him with both murders now?"

"Did you look closely at him in the interview room?"

Warwick thought carefully before answering. "Yes, looked tired and unshaven."

"And what would we expect to see on him?" He was toying with his young protege.

"I don't know Guv, what do you mean?"

They came to a stop just outside Rocke's office door for him to make his point.

"You saw Warshowski's body. He had been severely beaten, but the state of his knuckles meant he landed some serious blows too."

"And," asked a clueless Warwick?

"There's not a mark on Gus!" He turned and walked into his office, leaving that thought with the young detective.

"But he has got a ring missing."

"If he killed Warshowski, his face would be black and blue"

"Instead of just black?"

Rocke glared at his colleague with disapproval, which had the desired effect.

"Sorry, Guv."

"He is covering for somebody, Warwick, come on, surely you can see that?"

"But did he kill Helen?"

"I don't think so."

"So it was Warshowski who killed Helen, and then he gets killed for revenge?"

"That would make sense. Warshowski has no alibi because he didn't get back until 2.30am, so he has to be   the prime suspect for Helen's murder."

"Where do we go from here?"

"To the art college. I've set up a meeting with Professor "Doggy" Barker at 4.30, so we can see what he has to say for himself. Type up the interview and your notes from this morning and then we can wander up to the art college."

"OK, Guv."

Rocke went into his office, and Warwick returned to his desk and began to type up his notes. Rocke stood by the window, pondering over what had happened so far. Just then, his phone rang. It was Major Ratcliffe. He picked up the receiver.

"Rocke." He listened intently.

"Ah, Superintendent, Major Ratcliffe here."

"Yes Major, how can I help you?"

"Just spoken to our medic who has examined Warshowski's body. When we moved the body, we found his tie, which was obviously used to strangle him. There was also a large stone nearby which had blood on it, so that was used to hit him."

"And he had obviously been in a fight?"

"Yes," he confirmed, "some bruising to the ribs, and to the groin area, probably while he was on the ground."

"Well, we had one of our prime suspects walk into the station and confess to Warshowski's murder," he added with a hint of irony, which was lost on his American friend.

"That's great news," he replied happily.

"No, not exactly, Major. No obvious signs of a brutal fight with Warshowski. With the bruises and swelling on Warshowski's fists, he should have shown some signs of being in a fight."

"Then why confess, Inspector?"

"A good question, Major. He has explained in some detail how he arranged it, but it doesn't make sense. He is covering for someone, I think."

"Keep me up to date, Mr. Rocke."

"Not a problem, Major, will let you know as soon as we find anything out. Is there anything you need from us in the way of help with Warshowski?"

"Not for now, but thank you. Now find the killer for us."

"You have my word, Major. What time did Warshowski return to base?"

"He definitely returned to base at 02.30. Does that help?"

"Hmm. I will let you know. Speak to you soon."

"Thank you."

Rocke put the phone down and looked at Warwick.

"What did General 'Patton' want then, Guv?"

"More bruising on Warshowski's ribs which indicates he was kicked, probably when on the floor. Let's think about this for a moment. Warshowski is a big man. He was hit from behind with a rock, punched in the face, but obviously got some punches in himself on his attacker. On the ground, bleeding and probably dizzy from the blow to the head gets kicked in the ribs and the genitals too. This was vicious indeed."

"Totally different to Helen's murder, which was swift, yet not vicious."

"She knew her murderer, and I would suggest there was a relationship between them too."

"How can you say that?"

"In my experience, strangulation, face up, is a lover's revenge. They won't desecrate or mark the face, to disturb the beauty they love or lust after. Warshowski was revenge, a brutal and vicious attack from an irrational desire to kill. He did return to base at around 2.30am so he could have murdered Helen, and this is a revenge killing."

"So, we need to find out why Gus is lying to us?"

"Exactly, something isn't..." The telephone rang while Rocke was mid-sentence.

"Rocke .... Yes, hello Professor Barker." Rocke signalled to Warwick to pick the extension phone up and listen in.

"I believe you wanted to pop down and see me," Professor Barker said, "but I am actually free between lectures for a few minutes if I can help you."

"Ideally, I would like a face to face meeting later, is 4.30pm still OK for you?"

"It is a bit of a rush really," he said nervously, "as I am going into the theatre - part of the job, but someone has to do it! What's this about? How can I help you?"

"I believe you have a life model, Helen Smith?"

"Yes, lovely girl. She wanted to earn a few extra pounds of pocket money - you know how poorly nurses are paid, right?"

"How true, Professor."

"She's not in any trouble, is she? I thought she was a good girl?" He let out a nervous laugh.

Rocke deliberately didn't answer the question. "Did you see her the night before last?"

"Briefly in the Jac - but I didn't stay long. She was having a bit of a fight with one of the musicians and an American gentleman. I have to say I didn't like the look of that American. Most of them are good chaps, but he looked a bad sort!"

Rocke and Warwick exchanged glances. "What makes you say that?"

"He had his hands all over her, and she didn't like it. Gus wasn't too happy either, but it's none of my business what these girls get up to in their spare time. As long as they turn up when the students need them, that's fine with me."

"How long has she been with you?"

"Not with me, you understand," he said, carefully avoiding falling into one of Rocke's traps, "but she has been employed by the college for a few months I think, but I'd have to check for you."

"If you could find out for me, that would be very helpful. If we call at the college around 4.30 is that still OK with you, and we can talk further?"

"Sure... If I'm not there, I will be in the Crack."

"Great, see you later, thanks for calling."

Rocke put the phone down, and Warwick followed him seconds later.

"What do you make of that, then, Warwick?"

"Seems keen to help."

"Doesn't he?" he replied sarcastically. "Very helpful indeed. Nice man."

Warwick sensed there was more to that comment than a compliment.

"But?"

"Why call me at, what is it," he looked at his watch, "2.30 when we are meeting at 4.30 anyway? I got the feeling he wasn't too keen to meet and maybe deal with everything by phone?"

"So maybe he is a dirty old man?"

"Come on Warwick, I need rational thoughts, not immature stereotypes. Think a bit deeper than that. I think we should get down there earlier and rattle him, and just see what happens."

"Sounds good to me!" he said happily.

"Find out what you can about our Professor?"

"How?"

"You're supposed to be a detective, Warwick! Go and detect!"

Warwick was a little crestfallen at the accusation and sloped out of the room to return to his desk. He would show his boss who was a detective! He had a sudden flash of inspiration. He looked up the college number in the phone directory, sat in his chair and rang the art college. For once, his London accent might come in handy.

"Hello, this is Paul Warwick from the Times Newspaper. We are doing a feature on art in the provinces, and have heard about a tutor you have there, called Professor Barker. Is that right?"

"Yes sir, confirmed the receptionist."

"Great. I can send one of our local journalists to talk to him but just wanted to check a couple of details with you. How long has he been with you there?

"I'm not sure exactly, but seems like he's been here since it opened!"

"So that must be his whole career! He's only ever been at the college?"

"As far as I know, yes."

"Does he have a family?"

"No, never seemed to have time for a family."

"Really? ......the gay bachelor then?"

They laugh together.

"When could I send somebody to talk to him?" he asked in as friendly a manner as possible.

"He's already left the college for the afternoon as far as I know."

Warwick's demeanour changed very quickly.

"What do you mean left for the day?" he snapped, sounding too much like a policeman. "Sorry, I mean that is a shame. Do you know where he has gone?"

"I'm not sure, sorry."

"OK, not a problem, I will call you back. Thanks for your help." Warwick put the phone down and quickly ran into Rocke's office.

"Guv, just spoken to the college and Barker's left the building."

"What," he yelled, jumping put of his chair. "Why do our suspects like to do a runner?"

"Well he could always have walked in and confessed to something he didn't do!" he responded sarcastically, giving his boss a taste of his own medicine.

"As my good friend, Buddy said; That'll be the day! OK, let's get up to the college and see if we can find him."

They grabbed their coats and headed out into Hope Street and turned right, heading towards the art college which was only 500 yards up the road. They are passed by a couple of cars, but Hope Street is mainly filled with students walking up and down. Behind the art college, they see the cathedral, still under construction, rising into the cloudy sky. One middle-aged man stood out to them as he walked by, as he was wearing driving gloves, a flat cap and sunglasses. He looked so out of place with the students. Rocke and Warwick walked into the reception at the art college and went to the desk, where a young lady was sitting behind her desk typing. She noticed the two gentlemen.

"Can I help you?"

"Good afternoon, Miss," said Rocke politely. "I was calling to meet Professor Barker - is he in?"

"Sorry, you just missed him. You probably passed him on the street."

Rocke looked out of the door as if to see the Professor standing there. Maybe that unusually dressed man who caught their attention was Barker. Rocke decided to take a chance.

"My name is Detective Inspector Rocke. I wanted to talk to Professor Barker quite urgently if possible, but seems I've missed him. I left him with some papers, which are in his room, and I need to get them back now. Could you show me to his office by any chance?"

"Well, actually, I'm not supposed to..."

"Great, thank you, that is most helpful," he interrupted assertively. "Warwick, I think we may have just passed Professor Barker on the street."

Warwick caught on quickly.

"Yes Guv, I will go after him."

"Quick as you can, please Warwick. Even you should be able to catch him!"

Warwick ran out of the building and headed down Hope Street after Barker. Rocke encouraged the secretary to lead the way. She was still unsure, but Rocke was persuasive. They walked up a couple of steps, through double glass doors, and then headed up the marble steps of the flight of stairs on their left. They went passed the first floor and continued up to the second floor, where the secretary headed down a long corridor. Even though she knew the room was empty, she still knocked before opening the door. She held the door open for Rocke to walk in.

"Thank you, I won't be long; I will see you downstairs in a moment."

He made it clear that it was her time to leave, and she took the hint and headed down the stairs.

Chapter Eighteen

Love And Hugs

Rocke was alone in Professor Barker's room. He stood there, speechless for a moment. Before him, on every wall, were examples of the students' artwork, as well as stacks of canvasses on the floor, lined up like dominoes against a grey, metal filing cabinet. Under the desk was a pair of shoes, covered in mud. His desk was messy and disorganised, with papers and books everywhere. Rocke stared at the paintings on the walls again, and suddenly realised what he was seeing. They were classic paintings in the style of painters like Monet, Rembrandt, Picasso and many more, but all had one thing in common: the face was of the deceased girl, Helen Smith. The styles and artists were obviously different, but the muse was most definitely Helen.

Rocke examined a couple of the paintings and held one up by the string attached to the frame. He started to look at it more closely. 'Tough string, which if used to strangle a girl would leave the right type of marks,' he thought to himself. He noticed plenty of that particular type of string in the room, and a number of lengths of it cut already for frames. He picked a piece up, held it out taut as if to strangle someone, and was happy with that, so he put it in his pocket.

He looked under the desk and went back to that pair of shoes he had noticed with a significant quantity of mud on them. Rocke examined them closely. He started to talk out loud to himself.

"Been near any woods, Professor?"

He placed the shoes in a plastic bag that he found, in case they were needed as evidence.

Rocke looked through the shambles that was Barker's desk, and there, buried beneath the students' work, was a pink piece of notepaper, which stood out from the mountains of plain white ruled paper written in the students' scrawl. Rocke picked it up carefully, smelt the paper which was scented, and began to read.

'Dear Pops, thank you so much for your sweet letter. I can't thank you enough for the kindness you have shown me over these past months. The work I have been given is above and beyond what I could have expected, and you and the students have shown me great respect. At no point did I feel used or dirty, unless that Lennon started, but even he was polite, which surprised me greatly too.

'To think that I have found a place in your affection warms my heart. As I told you, I lost my grandfather at an early age, and don't have the closest relationship with my dad, so you have become my 'pop', a second father to me. When I needed an advance for the rent, you were there. If I needed a shoulder to cry on, you were there. When I told you about Gus, you helped me put everything in perspective and cope with my mixed emotions.

'Your devotion means so much to me, and your affection really touched my heart. However, dearest 'pops', the love I have for you is one of a grateful and adoring daughter, and I can't have a romantic feeling for my second father!

'I am flattered by your letter and your affection and will always be so grateful for all you have done for me. I think it is probably best that I stop coming into the college now as I don't want to put you in an awkward position or cause you any embarrassment.

Thank you so much

Love and hugs

Helly Belly

Xxx.'

The last few words were smudged, where the recipient had obviously cried over it. It was as if everything started to fall into place. This wasn't about a lover's tiff, but unrequited love. Now he had to hope that Warwick had done his job and caught up with the Professor. Spurred into action, Rocke put the letter into his pocket and headed down the stairs to the entrance hall. He caught the attention of the secretary.

"Thank you so much, I won't need to trouble you any further."

"Actually Inspector, that nice Mr. Warwick called to say he managed to catch up with the Professor, and they are planning to have a chat with him if you'd like to join them."

A smile came over Rocke's face - finally; he may have caught Helen's killer. Gus and his "confession" would have to wait. Rocke walked briskly out of the building and headed back down Hope Street towards the station. He now had to figure out how to carry out the interrogation, and when to reveal what he had found.

Chapter Nineteen

We've Got Him

Rocke walked down the corridor toward the interview room. Warwick was outside, obviously happy with himself.

"Well done Warwick. Any trouble?"

"No, he was just heading down the side street towards his car, which was parked at the bottom. I managed to catch up with him, but he didn't resist. He was almost resigned, to be honest."

"Excellent. I've got his motive in my pocket. Let's go get us a confession."

Rocke entered the interview room and sat at the table opposite Professor Barker, who was still wearing his sunglasses, flat cap and driving gloves. Rocke decided to go on the attack immediately and rattle his suspect.

"So Professor, can I ask you to take your sunglasses off, please?"

"I'd sooner leave them on if you don't mind."

"Actually, I do mind Professor Barker. Please, remove your sunglasses...now!" With that last word, Rocke bellowed the word 'now' while slamming the table with his fist! The Professor jumped with fright and removed his sunglasses. He revealed a cut on the bridge of his nose and severe bruising around his left eye. Warwick was shocked - Rocke wasn't.

"And now, if you'd like to take off your gloves, please?"

Warwick walked over to Barker and stood menacingly over him. A now totally subservient Barker slowly and carefully removed his gloves, wincing occasionally in pain. With the gloves removed, he was sporting severely bruised and swollen knuckles of both hands, probably with a number of broken bones.

"Now, Professor, do I need to go through the pain of extracting a confession, or will you take us through the process? By the way, I have read the letter from 'Helly Belly', so don't try to kid me."

With the mention of "Helly Belly", Warwick looked at his boss with a puzzled expression, not knowing what he was talking about. However, he was happy to observe. Without much time to think, Barker sighed and looked into the space in the corner of the room and then made eye contact with Rocke.

"I've no idea what you mean, Inspector," he said coolly.

"It's Detective Inspector actually, Professor," said Warwick, who seemed to be taking this personally.

"If we are going to use full titles it is," added Rocke, "or would you prefer I call you 'Doggy'?"

At that, the Professor bristled.

"How dare you," he exclaimed.

Warwick was shocked at what his boss had said. Was he trying to provoke the Professor? 'Maybe this guy is good at his job' he thought. He stepped forward again to make himself look threatening. However, Rocke was in control.

"That's OK, Warwick, not a problem. Now then, Professor Barker, I have read this letter from the victim, addressed to you, making it clear that your affection towards her was not reciprocated." With that, he placed the letter in front of the Professor for him to look at.

"I admit that I found her attractive, and we spent some happy times together, but that was all."

"So, how do you account for the injuries to your face and hands, which are consistent with being in a violent altercation?"

"I was mugged last night - somebody jumped me, and I fought them off but injured myself in the process."

"Oh, I am so sorry, that must have been frightening." He paused for a moment; the Professor relaxed, but Warwick knew what was coming. "So, I assume you reported this to the police?"

Barker was rattled. "Erm, I didn't want to waste their time; it was just a few knocks you know."

"Come on, Professor, do you really think I'm going to buy it?"

Rocke glared at Barker and made his opponent know that he wasn't going to be taken in so easily. There was a dramatic pause, while Rocke employed one of his most famous tricks. The first person to speak is the loser. His record was 20 minutes of complete silence: the person to speak first was the accused, and he confessed. He had no problem waiting for the Professor to crack, which he did, within 30 seconds.

"I didn't kill Helen, so look for somebody else."

"Who told you she had been killed? I never said that, did I, Warwick?"

"No Guv, you didn't, and neither did I."

Barker was taken aback because of his slip but quickly responded.

"Well, somebody must have told me. It was you in the phone call!" He pointed accusingly at Rocke, who simply shook his head in a very patronising manner.

"I never told you anything about Helen, so how did you know?"

"Somebody must have mentioned it in the college?"

Barker was beginning to sweat and fidget and started wiping his brow with the handkerchief from the breast pocket of his jacket. Rocke knew he had him rattled, so kept going, firing questions in quick succession.

"Were you in the Jacaranda the night before last?"

"Erm, yes, I do believe I was." He was desperately trying to stay calm but failing.

"And you witnessed the argument between one of the musicians and another man?"

"Yes, this American was having a go at Gus over Helen."

"So you know Gus, do you?" Sucker punch two, and he had him on the ropes.

"Erm, No, just heard his name."

"And where would you have heard his name?"

"At the Jac probably."

"You seem to know a lot without knowing anything."

"He is one of the musicians, isn't he?"

"When we spoke this afternoon, you said that you knew him. Warwick, what was the quote?"

Warwick took his notebook out and repeated the statement verbatim.

"He had his hands all over her, and she didn't like it. Gus wasn't too happy either, but it's none of my business what these girls get up to in their spare time."

"That tells me that you know exactly who Gus is - so why are you lying to me?"

"I must have forgotten - I know a lot of people."

"Where did you go the night before last, after you left the Jacaranda?"

"Straight home."

"Go home alone?"

"Yes, sadly, I am single."

"No witnesses, then?"

"Do I need some witnesses?"

"You might need them quite soon, Professor. You see; you had a relationship with the victim who was cut off by the victim, and then suddenly she turns up dead."

By now, the Professor was almost in tears, his voice trembling, though was it from guilt or fear?

"But I was nowhere near where she was found!"

"And where was she found?" Was this the knockout punch? Barker had slipped up again and was now becoming more and more nervous and stumbling over his words.

"Well, but.........erm............"

"And you followed Helen and you KILLED HER."

Barker lost his nerve and his temper and stood up and shouted emphatically.

"I DID NOT KILL HER!!!"

"Sit down, Barker," Warwick snarled, grabbing Barker by the shoulder and pushing him back into his seat. "We know you did it, so just confess and save us all a bit of time!"

Barker started to cry now and sobs the words out, "I didn't kill her, how could I kill her; I loved her?"

"So, you do admit to being in love with her," asked Rocke?

"Yes, yes, yes, she was sublime, serene, so beautiful."

"And when you couldn't have her, you decided that nobody else could either?"

"No, no, please believe me. I couldn't hurt her!"

"You're lying Barker!" shouted Warwick right into the Professor's face.

Barker suddenly stopped crying, and gave Rocke an icy stare - as if his personality changed from Jekyll to Hyde! His voice descended to a growl.

"Prove it, Superintendent! And I'm saying nothing more without my solicitor present!"

Rocke and Warwick were taken aback by this change in his manner, but Rocke had an idea.

"You've got some time to think about it, Professor."

Rocke stood up, and Barker put his head in his hands.

"Constable, take him to the cells."

Then, in full earshot of Barker, Rocke let Warwick know what he was about to do.

"Let's go and have a chat with Gus next door, shall we?"

Barker sat bolt upright and now looked scared. In an aside to Warwick he was pleased with the response.

"I think we have him rattled! I asked them to bring Gus into the next room for a chat."

"We need something concrete, Guv, because we've got nothing except circumstantial evidence on Barker!"

"I know, and when the solicitor arrives, he will be out of here!"

After exiting the room, they entered the second interview room. Gus was sat there nervously. Rocke and Warwick sat down and got straight into it.

"So, Gus, we've just been up to Burtonwood and looked upon the body of Corporal Warshowski. Tell me exactly how you killed him?"

"It doesn't matter."

"Yes it does, if only for the paperwork. I just need it in your words, then we can type it up; you sign it, and sort out the hangman for you. That OK?"

Gus suddenly realised what lay in store for him, and was wondering now if he should speak. His mind was whirring around, and he rubbed his hair in total despair. He decided to speak.

"Well, like I said, I went up to speak to a friend of my family."

"And who is that friend?"

"His name is Bobby Campbell." Warwick wrote the name down in his notebook.

"And he's a US serviceman?"

"Yes, sir."

"And what did you tell him to do?"

"To get Warshowski to come to the fence -
I've told you this. He came there, and I killed him."

"How did you kill him?"

Gus started to panic. "I hit him in the face; he
fell down, so I picked up a thick branch and beat him
around the head."

"Did he hit you?"

"No, didn't have a chance."

"And any other injuries you gave him?"

"Erm, well, I may have hit him in the arm
with the log too. His face was bleeding, and his eyes
told me he was dead. I left and came back to
Liverpool."

"Well, Warwick, what do you think? It makes
a good story, doesn't it?"

"Not quite Conan Doyle, sir."

"What do you mean," said a surprised Gus?
"I'm telling the truth."

"Warshowski did not die the way you
suggested."

"But.........."

"He was beaten on the back of the head with
a brick; he had broken ribs and had been brutally
kicked."

"But he said that.."
Suddenly, Gus paused, Realising what he had said.
Rocke had him too.

"You seem to have lost a ring, Gus?"

"Yes, I ...."

"But Warshowski was involved in a fight
with his murderer, and his murderer would have
received several punches in this fight. There is not a
mark on you, Gus."

"So, who is the 'he' you mentioned," interjected Warwick.

"I...................."

"If it helps, Gus, in the next room to you is Professor Barker."

Gus suddenly looked up - his demeanour changed completely.

"And we found a letter from Helen telling the Professor that she didn't love him, which drove him mad. Is Professor Barker the 'he' you were trying to tell us about?"

"You have him here," asked Gus?

"Yes, and we are about to charge him with the double murder of Helen and Warshowski, but we need your help."

Warwick was stunned by Rocke's comment. What was he playing at? He tried to catch the Superintendent's eye, but his boss had his eyes firmly fixed on Gus.

"You know he did it," asked Gus?

"Yes, but we need your help to prove it."

Suddenly, all Gus wanted to do was talk now.

"He said he was going to make me take the blame! He took one of my rings and said he would plant the ring by Warshowski's body if I didn't do what he said."

"So what did you have to do?"

"He came to me and told me that he followed Helen's taxi. Helen jumped out on Upper Parliament Street and ran towards Selborne Street. The Yank chased her but by the time the Professor had caught up and eventually found them in the alley, the Yankee boy had already raped her and killed her. He said he ran to the body as the Yank ran off into the night and found his dog-tags in Helen's hand. He brought the dog-tags to me as proof, with Warshowski's name on it. I was so angry I wanted revenge, but he said that wasn't the answer. He was going to talk to Warshowski and get him to hand himself in, but he didn't know how to do it. I told him that I had a friend up at Burtonwood - my auntie has a man friend there."

"Campbell?"

"Yes - Sergeant Bobby Campbell."

"And how were you to contact him?"

"Had to write a note, pass it in at the gatehouse."

"And what did you write?"

"Well, my writing ain't too good, see, so he had to write the note."

Rocke's eyes lit up, and he exchanged a knowing look with Warwick.

"What did he write?"

"He addressed an envelope to Campbell with a letter inside to Warshowski and just told him to meet him by the fence."

"And he would frame you?"

"Yes, said he would leave my ring by the body. Helen is dead, so I don't care anymore."

"But why should you hang for something you haven't done? Helen wouldn't want that."

"The Yankee man is dead, Helen is dead, an eye for an eye."

"But Warshowski didn't kill Helen."

Gus seemed visibly shocked with the news and worried that they might think that he was guilty. Again, Rocke used his 'first one to speak' rule and waited for Gus to keep talking.

"But you don't think I did it? I wouldn't hurt Helen!"

"That's not what the evidence tells us, Gus. It tells us somebody else was involved."

"Who did it?" Gus asked if looking for somebody somewhere to give him the answer.

Rocke let Gus think for a moment before he was hit by the realisation of who it was.

"Barker," asked Gus? "The Professor did it? However, he was in love with her too, he told me so."

"But she wasn't in love with him and told him that in a letter," explained Rocke.

"I thought he wanted revenge against Warshowski for killing the girl we both loved!"

"That's what he told you. He needed your help."

"But why?"

"To cover up his mess? I need to get back into the Professor soon, so if Warwick draws up the statement, we can sort you out later."

"But, what about what I did for him to get into Burtonwood? Will I be in trouble?"

"Don't worry about that for now. Constable, can you help this man back to his cell, please?"

Rocke stood up, shook Gus' hand, and Warwick followed him out. Gus was still confused and shell-shocked as the policemen left the room.

Rocke turned to Warwick.

"Can you chase up the fingerprints on the dog-tags? If we can find Barker's on them, it will all help! I'm going to speak to the Major in case Campbell kept the letter - if he did, and it is in Barker's handwriting, then we might have found the killer."

"You are definitely sure Gus didn't do it?"

Rocke said nothing and just looked at Warwick, giving nothing away.

"OK Guv, your call."

Warwick started to walk down the corridor, but Rocke called him back! He silently pointed Warwick in the opposite direction! With a grin, Warwick walked down the right corridor and headed for the forensic department. The office was at the far end of the corridor - he was still trying to find his way around! He found the door, knocked, and went in. It was a small lab, with microscopes, light-boxes and photographic equipment around. There was a row of filing cabinets along the far wall, and no windows in the room at all. Two men in white lab coats were in there, with their heads down. Warwick looked to find Ted Coleman, who he saw before. He was saved the embarrassment as Coleman looked up and spotted the rookie.

"Ah, it's Warwick, isn't it," he said charmingly?

"Yes. Hi Ted, I was wondering if you found any fingerprints on those dog tags?"

"Actually, there were quite a few on them. Too many really to identify any clear ones. Sorry, but I don't think I can help you."

"Damn, really hoped it would be clearer. Not to worry Ted, thanks for checking. It might have some handwriting to look at later."

"Ah, that is one of my favourite fields, forensic handwriting. Bring it to me as soon as you get it, and I will see what I can do for you."

"Thanks, Ted, will do. And thanks for helping the new boy!!"

They both smiled as Warwick walked out of the room.

Chapter Twenty

A Brief Conversation

Rocke decided it was time to pay another visit to Burtonwood airbase to find out more about this letter that was given to Campbell. He pulled up alongside Ratcliffe's building, parked the car and walked into the reception area. He was immediately shown into Ratcliffe's office where he was invited to sit down.

"Thank you for calling backup, Superintendent. What have you found out?"

"Well, Major, we believe that somebody passed a note into one of your men, asking Warshowski to meet his murderer by the fence, which he obviously did."

"Well, let's find him and clear this up."

"You have a Sergeant Bobby Campbell here? We believe it was he who received the note, which he passed on to Warshowski."

Ratcliffe saw this as an attack on his man and leapt to his defence.

"Hang on, Superintendent, are you trying to say that one of my men...."

"No, no, Major, don't misunderstand me. I believe that Sgt Campbell was tricked into passing the letter on to Warshowski, which led to his death. I am not accusing him at all, in fact; I need his help."

Ratcliffe calmed down again, as Rocke continued.

"If you can ask him if he still has the letter, that would help me immensely and might be the evidence I need to convict the murderer."

"OK, in that case, Superintendent, I will find Campbell now and see if we can get that letter for you."

He went through the door to his office and called for his assistant.

"Do you know where Sgt. Bobby Campbell is today?" The distant American voice that Rocke could hear replied.

"Will have to track him down, sir, but I don't know how long that will take."

"Quick as you can, please. Thank you."

"Sorry Superintendent, but it may take some time. Can I call you later when I have spoken to Campbell?"

Rocke stood up and shook hands with the Major.

"Thank you, Major. Between us, I believe we will catch Warshowski's killer and settle this for you quite quickly."

"Thank you, Superintendent."

Rocke left the office and returned to his car. It was a long journey for a two-minute conversation, but he knew he had to tread carefully, and it was so much easier to explain things personally.

As Rocke walked back into his office, and before he had sat down, Warwick knocked and walked in.

"Ah, Warwick, any good news on the fingerprints?"

"Afraid not, Guv. Far too many on there to distinguish any prints. What about the letter?"

"Major Ratcliffe is tracking down Campbell for us, so hopefully he can find that."

"If not, we've got nothing to hold Barker on."

"How is our Professor?"

"His brief has just arrived, so I expect we will be getting a call from him anytime now."

With that, the phone rang. They looked at each other and smiled.

"Rocke........Yes   Major,   thank you....................You   did?.....................................OK, thank you for calling and letting me know. I will let you know if we get any further here...........goodbye."

"Well,   good   news,   I   assume,"   asked Warwick?

"Yes, Campbell threw the letter away, but they started a search for it, and found it! He will get it down to us as soon as possible."

"What are we going to do next?"

"At the moment, we have Gus with a confession and lots of evidence, but the Professor looking like the guilty one!"

"So what do we do?"

"Be prepared to see Barker walking out of here."

The phone rang again.

"Rocke....... OK, on our way."

Rocke turned to Warwick.

"As if by magic, a solicitor appears! Come on Warwick, be prepared for a smug Professor!"

They exited the office and headed downstairs to the interview room.

As they opened the door, Barker was sat there innocently, and next to him was his solicitor. The solicitor was around the age of 55, with grey hair and dark-rimmed spectacles. He had a briefcase next to him, and a pen and pad on the table in front of him. Rocke and Warwick walked in and sat down. Before Rocke could speak, Carswell, the solicitor, addressed Rocke in a patronising manner.

"Right, you must be the policeman who incarcerates innocent people without evidence?"

"Good afternoon Mr. Carswell," Rocke said politely.

"Another assistant?"

"Ah, yes, DC Warwick, this is Horace Carswell, solicitor to the upper echelons, and some of the lower ones, of Liverpool society."

"And the most successful solicitor in Liverpool too, so I will be watching you Warwick, and I advise you now, don't cross me."

Warwick looked Carswell right in the eye and answered him confidently.

"And I would advise you, Mr. Carswell, that when you take on Rocke and Warwick, you better make sure that your clients' alibis are watertight, because if they're not, your reputation is worthless."

Rocke sniggered to himself. Carswell didn't know what to say to that for a moment, before changing the subject to his client.

"Are you charging my client with anything?"

"Not at the moment."

"Do you have any evidence with which to accuse my client of this heinous crime?"

"I don't wish to disclose anything at this moment while we pursue our enquiries. We can hold your client for up to four days if we want to."

"Charge him, or let him go, Rocke, because you could face a wrongful arrest allegation. Do you really want to face that? I would advise you to let him go."

"Yes, you're right, Horace. We've not got a case at the moment, but don't enjoy your freedom too much, Professor."

Barker turned to his solicitor, meekly. "Does that mean I can go, Horace?"

"Yes, I think you've spent enough time here, don't you?"

Warwick was not happy. Just then, there was a knock at the door. Rocke told them to come in. It was a constable who passed an envelope to him. He looked at the note attached to it and then carefully opened the envelope and placed the letter in front of Barker.

"Before you go, Professor Barker, take a look at this letter. Can you confirm this is your handwriting?"

He again looked startled, before quivering a quick, "No comment."

"This is the letter that was passed to Warshowski asking him to meet you to discuss the dog tags at Burtonwood. It wasn't on Warshowski's body but was in the rubbish at the base. Major Ratcliffe has just had it sent down to the station for me."

Warwick looked at the letter and then back at Barker. "Is this your handwriting, Professor?"

"We are not answering at this moment Inspector. I need some time with my client if you please?"

"Sure, we can give you some time. Come on Warwick, let's give them a chance to come up with a story. We've got examples of his handwriting, so it shouldn't be an issue!"

Rocke and Warwick walked out of the room, leaving Barker and Carswell to talk. Outside of the room, Rocke and Warwick could talk.

"So it was Barker?"

"Still circumstantial. We can't place him at the scene, and Carswell knows that. Still not enough to hold him."

"But Guv, do we really have to let him go?"

"Yes, I'm afraid so, Warwick. As well as that letter from Helen I found in Barker's room, there was a large quantity of string used to hang paintings, which would be perfect as the ligature used to strangle her. He also had muddy shoes."

"So why not ask him to explain those instead of letting him go?"

"Patience, Warwick, it is all circumstantial, and I don't want to reveal my hand yet. Let's go and see what story they have come up with."

"I'm still not happy, Guv."

"Trust me, Warwick."

Rocke knocked and entered the interview room again. Carswell spoke first. Rocke didn't even sit down but stood by the door.

"I've spoken to my client, and we aren't prepared to make another comment at this stage. Are you going to charge him?"

"Not at this stage, no."

"Then you have no right to hold him. Come on Professor, we are leaving."

Rocke turned to Warwick and spoke within earshot of Carswell and the Professor.

"And with letting Gus go as well, we need to talk!"

Carswell and the Professor took note of that last comment.

"You've let your other suspect go too? Dear, dear, George, you are getting desperate!"

Carswell laughed, while Barker grinned to himself. They walked out together still chuckling, leaving a bemused Warwick in their wake.

"You've let Gus go, Guv?"

Rocke checked to make sure the other two had left.

"Not yet, no. However, I'm about to."

"So, who did it? And why are we letting them both go?"

"Who did it and what we can prove are two different things. We don't have enough to charge either of them."

"But you're seriously going to let Gus go, again?"

"Yes, again."

Rocke walked out of the room, followed by Warwick, who was completely confused now.

"Oh, by the way, Warwick, I need you to follow Professor Barker and see where he goes. Don't let him out of your sight!"

Warwick suddenly smiled. "Yes, Guv!"

"Discreetly, please. Don't let him know you are there! I have a feeling he needs to make sure that he doesn't end up back in here."

"No problem, Guv, you can rely on me. I did a lot of this in London, quite successfully too."

"Quite successful isn't good enough - perfection please?"

Warwick smiled and headed swiftly for his coat so that he could catch the Professor. He ran down the stairs, wearing his trench coat with the collar up, but trying not to be too obvious. After all, he was the outsider and Barker the local, so he had to blend in. As he reached the entrance hall of the station, he saw Carswell and Barker on the street outside shaking hands and laughing, before going their separate ways; Barker heading towards the college, and Carswell turning back towards Hardman Street. Warwick slipped out of the police station and watched Barker, who was one hundred yards up Hope Street, approaching the art college. Warwick nipped in and out of doorways to make sure he wasn't seen: he was actually quite enjoying himself. Barker didn't look back as he felt that he was safe. As the Professor walked into the college, Warwick crossed Hope Street into Blackburne Place and hid on the corner of the road, able to see the entrance to the art college without being obvious. He pulled the collar of his coat up tighter as it was starting to get cold. He realised he could be in for a long wait, and remembered the part of the stake-out he didn't like.

Chapter Twenty One

The Confrontation

It was now late evening, and the sun was starting to set over Liverpool. A bored Warwick kept checking his watch every few minutes. He was finally stirred into action as he saw his target, Professor Barker, emerge from the art college. Barker headed straight down Mount Street in front of the Liverpool Institute building, and so Warwick started to follow him at a safe distance. The Professor walked all the way down to Berry Street and was now looking nervously around and constantly checking his watch. Warwick was on alert and was spying any suitable doorway into which he could dart should it be necessary.

Just then, Warwick noticed the fragrant smell of the nearby Chinatown wafting through the air, and he suddenly realised he was hungry. However, this was no time for food, as he had a fugitive to pursue.

Thankfully, so far, the fugitive in question had no idea he was being followed. As they reached Berry Street, Barker crossed over to the other side and turned right. Warwick reached the bottom of the road and looked carefully around the corner.

He spied Barker turning down Seel Street and quickly crossed the road to catch up with him. Again, looking carefully around the corner, he continued following Barker, nipping in and out of shop doorways, and between cars, occasionally kneeling down to tie a shoelace or give his prey the impression he was on his own. At the junction of Slater Street, Warwick just saw Barker turning right and disappearing from view, so he ran quickly to the corner of the street, and peered round the corner as if heading into the pub, where the noise of talking and laughing could be heard. There was no sign of Barker.

Warwick started to panic as he knew if he lost him, there would be hell to pay from his boss. He swore to himself and looked around at the buildings in front of him. Opposite him was what looked like an old warehouse, which was clearly boarded up, and he would have noticed Barker heading in there. There were a couple of shops, which were also closed with no lights on. Where could he have gone?

Warwick walked into the street and then suddenly realised where he was: outside the Jacaranda Club again. He walked slowly up to the front of the club, looked through the window and saw that the club was closed, which was strange. He peered through the window, but couldn't see anyone. However, he noticed that there was a dim light from the basement stairwell.

Warwick tried the door gently and found it open. He quietly turned the handle and made his way into the club. He could hear voices downstairs and crept over to the stairwell at the back of the darkened room. He walked down carefully, stair by stair so that he couldn't be seen or heard.

The basement of the Jacaranda was dimly lit, with just a solitary light above the stage area, where Gus was standing on the stage by his pans, with Professor Barker in front of him starting to argue.

"So what do you want, Prof," Gus asked dismissively?

"They are wanting to charge me with murder," yelled the Professor, shaking with nerves.

"They've got no evidence, have they? They are trying to blame me! My circumstantial evidence, plus the ring at the scene, and passing the note to Warshowski are all on me, not you?"

"But I didn't do anything," pleaded Barker, sounding as if he was ready to cry.

"I don't think you should be here, do you," said Gus calmly, yet assertively.

"What do you mean," he asked, sounding confused? "You asked me to come here?"

Gus suddenly sounded alarmed.

"Me? Why would I want you to come here?"

As if perfectly timed, from the snug at the side of the room, emerging from the darkness, appeared Rocke, Chief Constable Bell and Major Ratcliffe.

"Actually, that was me, Professor," said Rocke calmly.

Gus and the Professor were startled by Rocke's sudden appearance, and Barker started to panic, looking for an exit.   Then as an aside, Rocke shouted up the stairs.

"Er, Warwick, do you want to come down?" All eyes turned toward the stairs as Warwick appeared.

"How did you know I was here, Guv?"

"Don't worry twinkle toes," Rocke joked, "I was listening for you; they weren't!"

A sheepish Warwick walked across the room and stood at the bottom of the stairs. Gus suddenly became defensive, while Barker was in a real panic.

"What's going on here," Gus said innocently as if he didn't know what was going on?

"This isn't what it looks like," said Barker, pleading with the policemen to see he was innocent.

"What does it look like, Professor," said Rocke, trying another of his clever traps?

Yet again, Barker started babbling, right on cue.

"Well, I mean, erm, its, erm, I don't want to say anything without my solicitor present."

"You're not under arrest man, so calm down," snarled Gus, who then took his turn to plead his innocence. "But he's the murderer, isn't he? He was threatening me." Suddenly, the nervous, worried and heartbroken Gus was on show, fooling none of those present in the room.

"Let's have a look at some facts, shall we," said Rocke as he slipped into his Hercule Poirot mode?

Gus was suddenly worried and shut up. The Chief Constable, however, wanted to move things on, as did the accompanying Major.

"Come on Rocke, tell us what is going on," asked Bell?

"Let's see if I have this right, gentlemen. Please feel free to correct me if I am wrong."

He looked in the direction of the two suspects and was met with blank faces. He carried on with his summing up, much to the delight of the on looking Warwick.

"The Professor was infatuated with our victim, Helen, and had seen her in the Jacaranda that night and witnessed her arguing with Warshowski. He also has no alibi for the night. Warshowski was seen having intercourse with Helen in the alley; they were disturbed, and he ran away. She was strangled with a piece of picture-hanging string, of which there was a vast supply in Professor Barker's office."

"Hang on," interjected Barker, "don't start trying to frame me."

"Quiet, Professor," insisted Warwick.

"Carry on, sir," insisted Major Ratcliffe.

"The dog tags were in Helen's hand but were nowhere to be seen when we examined the body, or in the alley. However, they mysteriously appeared when Warwick examined the crime scene later that day. So, Professor Barker wrote a note which he handed into the airbase at Burtonwood, asking Warshowski to meet him at the fence, where he was subsequently killed. As Gus told us, Barker threatened to frame Gus by leaving his ring with the body and getting him to take the blame. Gus then confessed to the murder, but his explanation as to how he killed Warshowski was not accurate, which was clearly to implicate the Professor."

Warwick then stepped forward to arrest the Professor, but Rocke intervened.

"Hold on, Warwick, not so fast. One of the biggest problems I had was the colour issue. Warwick with his prejudices from London couldn't see passed the black guy for the murder, but I could only see he was being set up by somebody else."

Warwick hung his head in shame, trying not to catch the glare of Chief Constable Bell. 'If looks could kill', thought Rocke.

"Exactly," said Gus, "always blame the black guy! We are all criminals!"

Gus stared at Warwick, who was looking a bit embarrassed.

"The problem was," continued Rocke, "I too couldn't see passed the colour and couldn't believe that a black man COULD do it."

Gus was shocked, and his demeanour changed completely. Rocke walked to the middle of the room, between Barker and Gus, to conclude his summing up, as he took centre stage, with all eyes on him. Even Bell was surprised as this theatrical display.

"Let's take it from the beginning, examining what the evidence tells us. There was the argument here at the end of the night, witnessed by many people, then Warshowski and Helen headed off in a taxi. Gus came back in and was very angry. What we know is that Helen ended up in the alley behind Gus' flat, where she and Warshowski had sex up against the wall. She wasn't raped; it was consensual."

Barker gave a sigh of relief, but Gus was looking more worried, as Rocke continued.

"Warshowski was then scared by someone coming and ran off, leaving his dog tags in Helen's hand. Helen was attacked and strangled with a piece of string, which was extra strong, just like this."

Rocke produced a piece of thick string from his pocket, and carried on, clearly enjoying himself.

"This string is specially made for hanging pictures."

Warwick jumped in again.

"Just like in Professor Barker's office?"

"Exactly like that, Warwick. Professor Barker had several pictures of Helen on his wall; all hung using this string, and there was a large quantity of string in his office. Professor Barker also had muddy shoes under his desk."

Barker looked worried again and bleated, "But I didn't do it; I swear I didn't."

Rocke ignored him.

"You may have noticed that across from the Jacaranda is an art shop, R. Jackson & Son. I went in there earlier today, and they confirmed that last week, Gus went in there and purchased some string just like this."

As all eyes turned to Gus, who ran towards the stairs, but Warwick grabbed him and wrestled him to the ground, forcing him down and holding Gus' arm behind his back, while Warwick placed his knee on the backside of his suspect. Gus tried to wrestle free, without success.

"Gus killed both Helen and Warshowski. Warwick, do the honours please?"

"With pleasure. Gus Woodrow, I am arresting you for the murders of Helen Smith and Chuck Warshowski. You   are not obliged to say anything, but what you do say may be put into writing and given in evidence."

Gus struggled and grunted while the caution was being read to him.

"So it wasn't the Professor," asked Bell? "Tell us what happened, Rocke?"

"Gus realised that, with the string, he could frame Barker. I assume, Professor, that Gus was blackmailing you over your affection for Helen?"

Barker now realised that it was nearly at an end, and was happy to talk.

"Yes, he said I had to help him, or he would tell the college, and I would lose my job! However, how did you know it wasn't me?"

"One of the giveaways was when we first met, I realised you were left-handed. Helen was struck behind the right ear, showing that our attacker was most likely right-handed. By coincidence, when we examined Warshowski's body, the knuckles of his left hand were much more swollen and bruised than his right hand, which was hardly marked. Warshowski was also left-handed, so if he had punched you, you would have had bruising under your right eye, not your left eye, so you must have been punched by a right-handed assailant. Therefore..."

"The murderer had to be a right-hander," said Warwick.

"Exactly. Gus went to the alley and came across the couple having intercourse, and when Gus appeared, Warshowski ran away. In his anger, Gus hit Helen over the head and then strangled her. When he realised what he had done, he saw the dog tags and the quarters and the opportunity to frame Warshowski. However, he couldn't let Warshowski live because he would have known that the man chasing them in the alley was a black man. He had to get rid of Warshowski next and, with the Professor's help, sent a note to somebody he knew at Burtonwood, Sgt Campbell, and lured Warshowski to the fence where he killed him."

"But what about the bruises and cuts on the Professor, Guv?"

"Gus threatened the Professor and beat him up to keep him quiet, isn't that right Professor?"

"Yes," he said, his voice still trembling, "I had to do what he said, or he said he would kill me! When I tried to argue, he hit me and told me if I said anything else he would finish me off. I tried to hit him, but I'm no good; I've never been in a fight in my life. I missed him and hit the wall and the floor with my fists."

Warwick couldn't help but smirk to himself at this pathetic little man in front of him. Rocke noticed but carried on.

"When we finished with Gus at the station, I shook his hand and saw him wince as I squeezed his knuckles."

Warwick recalled his boss shaking Gus' hand, and thought it strange at the time. Now it made sense. He listened even more intently as his boss continued to present his evidence to his attentive listeners.

"As well as shaking his hand, I also noticed a slight friction burn on the skin between the thumb and index fingers of both hands, which will be the friction burns from the string where he strangled Helen. I think if we turn the lights on..."

As if he were the junior, Bell duly went over and switched the main lights on.

"Gus' knuckles on the right hand, I think you'll find Warwick, are now showing signs of bruising?"

Warwick looked at Gus' hand and he saw some mild cuts with considerable bruising and swelling coming through, plus the friction burns exactly where Rocke said they would be.

"I'm sure we will find more injuries to his ribs when we examine him, which will be on his right-hand-side, as Warshowski was left-handed."

Warwick gave Gus a dig in the ribs, making him yell out indistinguishable expletives as he lay there in pain!

"Also," continued Rocke, who now addressed the prostrate suspect, "since we first met on the morning after the murder, you have developed a slight limp, meaning you probably injured your leg in your fight with Warshowski. He was kicked in the body and the groin, and I guess you have broken a couple of toes too."

There was no reaction from Gus. Rocke turned his attention back to his colleagues.

"The ring wasn't planted by Professor Barker because it came off during the fight with Warshowski. If you look where the ring should have been on his finger, there is a small cut below the knuckle where it was pulled off and ended up beneath the dead body of our American. When Gus realised the ring was missing, he had to come up with a plan, so he confessed to a murder he actually did, pretending that he didn't, and when we pushed him for the details of how he did it, he deliberately gave us the wrong information to fulfil his plan of framing Professor Barker, and we almost fell for it. I was too colour blind."

Rocke was obviously angry with himself at having been taken in.

"He was then going to murder the Professor, but we arrested him and messed up his plans."

Professor Barker turned to Gus in bemusement.

"How could you do it? How?"

Finally, Gus snapped and even though he could hardly move on the floor, he snarled at Barker.

"She was mine, not yours, and certainly not that Yank's! How dare he turn her head and show me up in front of my friends? I told him outside not to take her. After work, I went home and found them in the alley. I see the Yank with Helen pinned against the wall. I thought he was raping her..."

"But he wasn't, was he?" Rocke asserted sharply. "She consented didn't she, Gus? Didn't she?"

"He must have said something to her, or why did she try to get to my flat?"

Rocke suddenly became angry!

"But she consented! Two adults consenting to have sex!"

At the word 'sex', Gus started to wriggle and try to release himself from the grip. Warwick was not about to let that happen.

"You may not like it, Gus, or approve, but it was their right, not yours!"

Gus continued to struggle in vain on the ground, but Warwick gripped him even more tightly.

"She was mine: mine!" he continued to protest. "She loved me and was better than some quickie against a wall - my wall! She was running to my flat for safety, but I couldn't save her."

"No, she wasn't. Her friend Dot was with Sammy, so she was going to look for her and maybe go into his flat, not yours. So did you shout at them?"

"No, I crept at first but then started to run. They were startled and he pulled up his trousers, dropped the coins, and ran away like the cowardly Yank that he is. She started to run too."

"But why hit Helen?"

"She laughed in my face! How dare she laugh in my face? It was all a game to her - she just saw it as sex, not love."

"So you hit her?"

She turned her back on me to straighten her dress, and I lost it! I just grabbed something from the alley and hit her on the head. She fell upon the ground, and I strangled her with the string in my pocket. She looked sorry in her eyes! I then saw the dog tags in her hand and planted them there so you would think the Yank did it."

Warwick had a question.

"But if this was not pre-meditated, how did he have that string from the art shop?"

Rocke looked over to the small stage.

"Gus uses it for securing his steel pans to the frame."

"It's the best there is," Gus said proudly, not realising that he was making it worse for himself, not that he cared anymore. "I had been using some that evening, so it was in my pocket."

They look over to the instruments on the stage and can see the string still holding the pans together.

"And that is when you decided to frame the Professor. I examined the string before and that piece there," said Rocke as he walked over to the piece of string on the pans, "contains small flakes of skin which I am sure will confirm that it is the murder weapon. After you had realised that Barker used the same string when you visited his office, you saw the perfect opportunity to frame him. You went to Barker, told him Warshowski had killed Helen, and that you wanted his help to get your revenge. You forced him into writing the note and took it to Burtonwood to lure Warshowski to the boundary, as you had his dog tags, which he had lost in the alley. With the letter in the Professor's handwriting, you thought it was a dead cert that we would arrest him."

"Exactly," said Gus, "his handwriting, not mine."

"Maybe, but it was your letter!"

"It should have been in Warshowski's pocket, but it wasn't. However, I knew the fool would need his dog tags back, so I could get rid of the Yank and the Professor too because they both took my girl!"

"Actually, Gus, the letter was found at the base, and it was in the Professor's handwriting. Major Ratcliffe found it and brought it here for me. The letter was written under duress in your attempt to frame the Professor. It didn't work!"

"It was in his handwriting!" he continued to claim.

"Yes, also written left-handed, so we know it is his writing. However, let me read it to you, shall I? It may have been in his handwriting, but you dictated it. It says: 'Warshowski, no Yank is gonna take no girl away from me. You done her wrong so meet me by the perimeter fence at point B, and you'll get your dog tags back and sort this mess.' I think it is safe to say that somebody with the Professor's education would never structure a note like that using colloquial language and with so many grammatical errors! In every conversation, the Professor has always referred to Warshowski as an American, but you are the only one to call him a Yank! He reproduced it exactly as you dictated it - as if it was in your own handwriting. And who else would know the exact meeting point at the base, point B, except somebody who had a good knowledge of the base? The only other possibility was that the Professor tried to fake the letter, but he didn't have any understanding of the terminology he would need to use to frame you. I needed you to confirm that though, so thank you."

Rocke held up the letter, which was inside an evidence bag.

"Also, on examining the letter, there are traces of oil on it, similar to the grade of crude oil found on the oil drums from which Gus makes his pans. I noticed you often have dried oil under your fingernails. The paper is also exactly the same quality and colour as the sheet of paper on the stage on which you have written your set list, and has a Dandy roll watermark, which is only visible when applying some watermark fluid."

Rocke took a small bottle of fluid from his pocket.

"You foolishly used the next sheet of paper down from a previous set list, as it left an imprint of the songs you had played that night, which become visible when you hold it up to the light. The pen you gave to the Professor is the same one you used to write your set list! It all comes back to you, Gus. It might be the Professor's handwriting, but all this paper says to me is that you are guilty. I'm pretty sure that when we dust it for fingerprints, we will find yours on it."

"You think you're so clever, don't you? I don't care what they do to me!"

"And I assume that you were going to kill the Professor as soon as you had the opportunity?"

"Of course, and then leave this town for good!"

"It wasn't even reciprocated, love! It was lust, control and infatuation, a deadly combination."

"I think we've got enough for a conviction, Rocke," said Bell proudly. Rocke looked satisfied.

Warwick managed to get Gus to his feet roughly, and though Gus tried to wriggle, it was more in submission, as he knew he couldn't escape.

"Thank you, Inspector," said Major Ratcliffe, "you've done the US Air Force a great service, and I thank you. Warshowski wasn't a saint; I know that."

"But he didn't deserve to die, Major."

"Exactly. Thank you." Ratcliffe shook Rocke's hand firmly and walked up the stairs.

"Well done Rocke," said Bell proudly, as he patted him on the shoulder.

"If you give people enough rope, sir," Rocke said, as he held up the incriminating piece of string, "they'll hang themselves!"

"But this time," replied Bell, "someone else will be doing the hanging for him."

The Professor was stunned, but relieved, and had a tear in his eye. He walked over to Rocke.

"You know what, Inspector? I don't care about my job anymore. I think I need a break."

"It has been an ordeal, and sorry we had to put you through it, but we had to follow the evidence."

"That's OK, just doing your job. An innocent girl, gone forever. She was so beautiful and free, with her whole life ahead of her, and we poisoned her - all of us. Poor girl."

Barker walked off upstairs, giving one last look at Gus, while Warwick followed him up the stairs with Gus in handcuffs.

Bell turned to Rocke.

"Well George, that was a fine piece of detective work."

"Thank you, sir, but I was stupid. All I could see was Warwick's prejudice, and I was too blinkered. I even let him walk free at the start! He nearly got away with it, and we almost charged the wrong man!"

"But you didn't, and that is what matters. We should all learn something from every case, and maybe you will be a little wiser after this one?"

"This was never about colour, creed, nationality or anything like that. It was lust, love and revenge - pure and simple. Maybe I was just too colour-blind to see it?"

"Well, I'd say you've got twenty-twenty vision now George!"

"Yes, sir. Now, I've got to go and see Helen's parents."

They walked up the stairs into the club. Bell patted Rocke on the back once more.

Chapter Twenty Two

Be Careful What You Say

A Liverpool Echo reporter and a photographer had been ushered into Chief Constable Bell's office where, along with Bell, Rocke, Warwick and McKenzie were at the end of an interview.

"So, Chief Constable Bell, you can reassure the public that the streets of Liverpool are safe again?"

"When you have a team like I have," Bell said proudly, "then we will ensure that the streets of Liverpool will always be safe."

"Now, can we have a photograph of the four of you?"

They lined up along the wall like a firing squad, uneasy and awkward. The photographer lined them up and got them to relax more, and took a couple of photographs.

"Let me make sure I get your names right," said the reporter. "It's John McKenzie, the Police Surgeon, Detective Constable Paul Warwick, Detective Inspector George Rocke...that's R.O.C.K.E. and Chief Constable Richard Bell."

"That's it, thank you," said Bell proudly. "Warwick, can you show the gentlemen out?"

Warwick walked out with the reporter and the photographer.

"So, is Bell a bit uptight?" the reporter said to Warwick. "Seems a serious type of guy."

Warwick was a little unguarded in his response and should have known better.

"No, he's alright really. He's known around here as 'Ringer' you know? 'Ringer' Bell!"

"Ha ha, love it," said the reporter, making a mental note of that comment.

Warwick chuckled to himself as they walked out, oblivious to any damage he might have done.

Chapter Twenty Three

Foot In Mouth Disease

Rocke was sitting down at his desk, enjoying a cigarette and glass of whisky, when Warwick wandered in.

"Well, Guv, that was a neat piece of detective work. It really was Gus after all."

"Yes, just couldn't see it at first."

He poured Warwick a glass of whisky, as he took his seat.

"I could, but probably not for the right reasons."

"Well, I hope you've learnt from this case, as I certainly have."

"I have, and I know I have to look again at my prejudices, but I think one thing remains the same."

"Which is," said Rocke, curious as to what the punch line was going to be?

"People should stick to their own colour, their own type. Helen and Gus tried to mix it, but it didn't work. I just think you're messing with trouble with a mixed marriage."

"You think so?"

"Yes, nothing against coloureds or whites, but if we stick to our own, life is simpler. Some of these coloured girls can be pretty, I agree, but I will stick to my own, thank you."

Just then, Warwick watched an elegant black woman walk in, accompanied by one of the constables.

"You see, even your coloured prostitutes are pretty, but you shouldn't mix it up."

The lady walked up to Rocke and gave him a kiss upon the cheek. Warwick was stunned into silence.

"DC Paul Warwick, I'd like to introduce you to my wife, Emily Rocke."

Warwick's mouth was open, and his face was flushed with embarrassment! He didn't know where to look.

"Catching flies, Warwick? Or is that the Birkenhead tunnel I can see?"

Warwick snapped out of it as Emily extended her hand to him.

"Erm, Emily, Mrs. Rocke, nice to meet you. So you're ...."

"Mrs. Rocke, George's wife, but you can call me Queenie."

"He can," asked Rocke?

"He can," she confirmed.

"Queenie? Why Queenie?" he asked, trying to make amends. "Is it an old African tradition or are you a tribal princess?"

She laughed, and Rocke wasn't sure whether to laugh or punch him.

"It's because her initials are ER, just like her majesty!"

Everyone except Warwick laughed, as his face turned a lovely shade of crimson, and every eye turned towards him. Suddenly, the penny dropped and he laughed too: he knew he had been caught out again. Rocke looked at Warwick and knew he didn't mean any harm by his previous comments, ignorant, though they were.

"OK, Queenie, you're ready," he asked as he sprung to his feet? He looked over to his new colleague.

"Good chat Warwick, and maybe we can catch some more baddies tomorrow?"

Rocke extended his hand and Warwick shook it firmly. Rocke took his wife's hand and they walked out together. Warwick slumped into his chair and buried his head in his hands. How could he have been so stupid?

Chapter Twenty Four

I Read The News Today, Oh Boy

Bell was sitting in his office and picked up the morning paper. His face turned purple as he shouted through the office.

"Rocke! Warwick! Get in here now!"

They both stopped what they're doing, looked at each other and headed to Bell's office as fast as they could.

"What's going on," Rocke asked?

"Beats me," Warwick said.

They entered Bell's office to see an enraged Chief Constable.

"What's up, sir? Another murder?"

"It might be. Who has been talking out of turn to the papers?"

Rocke looked to his colleague, who answered for them both. "Don't know what you mean, sir."

Bell picked up the newspaper and turned it around to show Rocke and Warwick the headline which made them erupt with laughter.

The caption in big letters below the photo taken in Bell's office of John McKenzie, Paul Warwick, George Rocke and Bell said:

"*John, Paul, George and Ringer*"

And the headline was:

"*Mystery of Pretty Nurse of Penny Lane Solved*"

Rocke looked at Warwick, who was blushing. Bell ordered them out of his office.

"If it helps, sir, I think the name rings a bell!"

With that, Bell threw the newspaper at the two policemen as they ran for safety. When they reached Rocke's office, they collapsed into their seats, still laughing.

"Well, Warwick, that was a day in the life of a Liverpool policeman. Think you'll stick around?"

"You know what Guv, I think I might do that." They clinked their glasses together, said cheers, and took a quick sip before they again heard the booming voice of their Chief.

"Rocke!"

"Here we go again, Warwick," he said as they downed their drinks quickly, and headed back across the office to be handed a new case.

ROCKE will return in his next Liverpool story, "Long Tall Sally", soon.

Check out the website for location photos and evidence from "That'll Be The Day", plus news about the new stories coming soon:

www.inspectorrocke.com

About The Author

In 2000, after being signed off from work on medical grounds, I began a quest to discover as much as I could about The Beatles and Liverpool. Since then, I have written three books on the early history of The Beatles, collaborated with official Beatles biographer Hunter Davies on another Beatles book, am working on other Beatles books and television documentaries too.

Having interviewed numerous people, both connected with The Beatles and social historians, I have amassed an incredible knowledge of Liverpool in the late 1950s and early '60s. With my other passion being detective stories and television programs, I decided to created a 'factional world' containing some fictional characters along with the some factual people, all set within actual places related to the early history of The Beatles in Liverpool.

David Bedford

More about David:

Website - **www.davidabedford.com**

Facebook - **www.facebook.com/davidbedford**
@liddypooldave

Twitter - **@liddypooldave**

Instagram - **@liddypooldave**

www.ingramcontent.com/pod-product-compliance
Lightning Source LLC
Chambersburg PA
CBHW032020050726
47590CB00006B/2244